Con Quest!

Quest!

SAM MAGGS

【Imprint】
MAKE YOUR MARK
New York

[Imprint]
MAKE YOUR MARK

A part of Macmillan Publishing Group, LLC
120 Broadway, New York, NY 10271

Library of Congress Control Number: 2019948845

ISBN 978-1-250-30727-9 (hardcover) / ISBN 978-1-250-30728-6 (ebook)

Our books may be purchased in bulk for promotional, educational,
or business use. Please contact your local bookseller or the Macmillan
Corporate and Premium Sales Department at (800) 221-7945 ext. 5442
or by email at MacmillanSpecialMarkets@macmillan.com.

Book design by Elynn Cohen

Illustrations by Chris Danger

Imprint logo designed by Amanda Spielman

First edition, 2020

10 9 8 7 6 5 4 3 2 1

mackids.com

Whoever steals this book from me
Shall face a fate worse than death:
Forced to watch every cursed movie
On repeat 'til their last breath!

To the wonderful friends
I've met at conventions,
And to all the ones I've yet to meet.
Stay nerdy.

1

Cat saw an opening and pushed forward, squeezing between a very tall, very pregnant, costumed lady and someone in full-body futuristic space armor. The pregnant lady angled herself to the side to let Cat slide past.

"Thanks!" Cat said as she forged ahead. She loved comic book conventions. *Loved* them. But she *didn't* love being late, and if her family would just hurry up, then maybe—

Her cape tightened around her neck and Cat was yanked backward, bouncing like a pinball off the space soldier's flimsy plastic shell and the costumed lady's thigh.

"Cool ricochet," said Cat's twin, Alex. He

hadn't even looked up from his handheld console, and now he was using their brand-new vocab word to tease her? Cat stuck her tongue out at him. Alex didn't even seem to notice. He was similar to Cat in so many ways physically (dark hair, hazel eyes, typically Italian features like their dad, a love of graphic tees and jeans), but personality-wise they could really be total opposites.

"Slow *down*," snapped Cat's older and much stronger sister, Fi, dropping her hold on the back of Cat's cape and returning to fidgeting with her coffee-stained, leopard-print blouse. Who knew being a varsity soccer player at fourteen could get your biceps that buff? Fi had definitely gotten all the height in the family. She was tall and muscular, her thick brown hair almost always pulled back with a scrunchie. Most days, she was in an oversized vintage tee, denim shorts, and sandals. Her favorite accessory was a refillable metal water bottle. She tried very hard to know as little about anime as she could. Today, though, Fi was at a nerd convention and had traded shirts with their mother during a last-minute hot beverage–related elevator disaster. Cat knew her sister was miserable.

Cat yanked her costume back into place. She'd been poring over screencaps of her favorite anime online for months to get the details just right for this convention, but honestly it was held together by a safety pin and a wish. Plus, they were still so, *so* running late. Didn't Fi understand? Didn't anyone understand? Why couldn't everyone else just keep *up*?

GeekiCon, the largest comics convention in the world, had been a regular event in Cat's life since she could remember—at least five years. Well, she'd been coming since birth, really, so the six years before that, too, but she couldn't remember those ones. (She was a baby. Obviously.) Her parents, Anna and Luca Gallo, were famous for writing this comic called *Ducky McFowl* that had been turned into an animated series in the '90s and now had this massive cult following that Cat didn't really understand. Cat was used to people squeezing into sweaty, crowded rooms to hear her parents talk. Sometimes she even watched their recorded panels online afterward, so she could spot herself and Alex in the audience making faces at the camera.

Sorry, Cat mouthed, backing away from the lady in costume. In response, the woman bowed her head and brought her gold wrist cuffs together with a wink. Her way of saying *Don't worry about it* without needing words.

"Mom," Cat said, turning around to walk backward while getting her parents' attention. "Your panel starts in five minutes!"

"These things, they never start on time, *môj miláčik*," her mom said in the thick accent Cat was way over being embarrassed by. Cat thought it was actually really cool that even though English was her mom's second language, she managed to kick butt by writing one of the most successful comics of all time. It made her feel a little better when people made fun of how her cabbage noodles smelled when she brought them for lunch at school.

Cat's mom pushed up her glasses as she scanned the crowd—a vantage point Cat didn't have. Anna Gallo's shoulder-length hair was tinted a dark burgundy, a color that set off her always-kind gray eyes. Her favorite silver necklace—the little Celtic knot she'd bought with Cat at Seattle Comic Expo—glinted on top of her black sweater. "We will be fashionably late," she said decisively.

Cat almost rolled her eyes and then remembered her mom would dock a dollar off her allowance for attitude. Alex didn't bother looking up from his console but he still smirked at Cat. She knew *he* knew how close she was to losing her chill.

"She's right, kiddo—we're almost there," Cat's dad agreed, squinting at the crowd through his glasses. Her dad hated crowds, but he loved talking in *front* of crowds, so he struggled through it for the fans.

"Exactly," Julie, her parents' publicist, called back from the head of their little pack. She was a very cool and *very* talented Korean American lady who always showed Cat pictures of her gigantic fuzzy dogs during convention weekends. And she could throw elbows to push through a crowd like no one else.

But please! What did "fashionably late" even mean anyway? Probably nothing. Probably just something her mom made up. Some weird phrase that didn't translate right from Slovak. They weren't even fashionable. The only one who cared about clothes was Fi, who had her arms crossed over her stomach and wore a scowl like that one *Vigilante League* member who had laser eye beams. Fi would decimate everyone in this con if she could.

Cat should just accept lateness was kind of

their family's thing—Mikaeyla Xu's family had their nightly sit-down dinner and Amelia Wilson's family had their weekly argument over something trivial. But Cat's family was just . . . *late*, all the time, and when the five of them finally managed to make their way into a room, people always noticed.

"Coming through!" a guy in a giant suit of foam armor called as he nearly slammed an oversized elbow pad into Cat's head. She dodged, barely, and felt Alex grab her hand, tugging her in the opposite direction of the cosplayer.

"You should really be paying more attention," Alex said. It was the first time she'd seen him look up.

"Me? You're the one with your eyes glued to your screen," she said, pointing to his console. "I *was* paying attention, I was almost through when—"

"Cat! Left to the escalators!" Fi barked. Everyone near them turned to look, including the three people dressed as full animals. Cat waved Alex forward and grinned at Fi. Her older sister might hate it here, but she knew her way around this convention center better than any of them.

"You heard her, Mom, let's go!" Cat called,

Alex following behind her, ahead of the rest of their family.

They squeezed onto the big escalator in the convention center's atrium and Cat finally got to take it all in. You know that look people get on their face when they talk about their favorite place in the world? Like when Cat's dad talked about growing up in the woods of Minnesota and the crisp air and smell of pine and the way the colors of the leaves change? That look was Cat's entire brain at GeekiCon.

It was three whole days wandering the convention's main floor full of booths and stalls, checking out everything from the smallest Artist Alley table to the massive anime setups to all the amazing costumes people had spent hours and hours making *themselves*. Sure it was hectic, but it was a place where people got to be their geekiest selves, where obsessions didn't get you teased . . . where you just got to *be*.

Cat looked up with awe at the gigantic WEL-COME TO GEEKICON banner hanging over the convention center's atrium. She held up her phone and snapped a selfie with her and Alex just visible beneath the logo. This was the best con in the world, and they were finally back.

And this year, it's going to be the best con ever, Cat thought, smiling at her perfect framing on the WELCOME TO GEEKICON selfie.

Because this year, she was going to win the Quest.

2

People.

So many people.

Not that people were a bad thing, generally, but they were everywhere. That was the thing about GeekiCon: thousands of *people*. In costumes, in character, all brushing past him.

And it wasn't just inside the convention center. Alex had been to a few other cons around the country with his folks and the thing about *those* cons is that when you leave those cons, well . . . you've *left the con*. You go outside and after you walk a block or two it's just normal, really. Just normal Seattle or New York or Chicago or wherever you happen to be for the two or three weekend hours when you're not inside the gray concrete walls of the convention.

Which means fewer people.

But this con was *not* like that. Alex swatted at Cat's hand so she'd stop interrupting his game.

Adventure of Zenia took some serious concentration. It was a single-player game where your character wandered through the wilderness in search of ancient temples. Getting through the temples took a lot of tough puzzle-solving and it wasn't for the faint of heart. This was something like the fifteenth *AoZ* game, and Alex loved each one more than the last.

Alex clutched his console in sweaty hands and stared down harder into it, trying desperately not to think about the number of people around them, watching Cat's feet go one in front of the other just out of the corner of his eye. He couldn't lose her.

He almost tripped trying to avoid touching someone. The first of many times this weekend, he knew.

Earlier this morning, after Alex had finally located his favorite pencil (which he couldn't find anywhere until Fi discovered it behind the couch, and he went *nowhere* without his sketchbook and pencils, so this was very important), he left his hotel room and crowded into an elevator with his whole family and a guy dressed in a red spandex unitard. (He pulled the look off, in Alex's opinion.) Before Alex knew it, his family was in a lobby decorated with bright *Vigilante League* decals, and the front desk guy was wearing a Captain Patriot T-shirt under his uniform blazer, and when Alex walked out onto the street, every restaurant had a GeekiCon–themed menu and every person was wearing a costume and most of them hadn't even bought them at a Hot Topic. Yes, to most geeky kids, this is what the center of the universe would feel like—if the center of the universe was actually cool and not just a gigantic ever-expanding void, which is a thing Alex had just read about on Wikipedia—but he already had a hard enough time processing the everyday world. Processing the everyday world—the words his therapist used to explain the challenge of being autistic. When Alex got worked up, he felt like he had to just . . . close up inside himself and definitely not touch anything. That's when sometimes his dad's voice would get soft, just like it did now.

"Buddy," he said, crouching down next to Alex. "Need a minute? Just a little sensory overload, right?" Alex wasn't looking at him, but he knew that his dad's eyes would be all crinkled up behind his glasses. At this distance, Alex could have seen all the little gray bits in his dad's short black hair and beard. Alex liked those bits. He concentrated on them sometimes while having conversations.

Alex kept his eyes glued to his console and nodded. All *that*—the pencil and the elevator and his mom's coffee spill and the *people*—had happened even before they got to the convention center. Which is where they were now. No escape. But Alex knew he was here for a greater purpose. The greatest purpose of all, really. So he lifted his head and looked his dad square in the eyes.

"I'll be okay," Alex said, projecting a false confidence he didn't even know he could fake. "I just need to get into the panel room and take out my sketchbook. Or play more *AoZ*."

"You got it, kiddo." His dad smiled and stood up, knowing better than to touch Alex in moments like this. "Let's rock and roll."

Alex took a deep breath as he hopped off the escalator. Doodling always managed to chill him out. *Soon.*

GeekiCon staffers ushered their family forward through the convention center's second floor. Long hallways lined with doors upon doors, all leading to their own gigantic panel rooms. Suddenly, Alex felt he was deep in the belly of the whale. He'd read that happened to a guy once in a really old story. (Gross.) That's what it felt like here, shoved into a big belly of a hot, sweaty, stinky animal and jostled around with the rest of its stomach contents.

Alex knew he wasn't making this sound pleasant. He'd watch the way his mom's face would change when he described things this way, so he tried not to. He tried not to even think about any of it.

Think nicer things. Try to make eye contact. Here for a good reason.

Alex was a little spoiled, and he knew it; with his parents' PROFESSIONAL badges and Julie, their publicist, he and his sisters never had to wait in line to get into cons. But what with the losing-the-pencil fiasco this morning, and then Fi changing her outfit nine times, and Dad misplacing the hotel key, and Mom spilling her latte on her blouse and having to swap shirts with Fi in the elevator, they were cutting it pretty close on making it to their parents' panel.

"Hey, Alex," Cat said suddenly. Alex looked up to find Cat's phone was being shoved into his face. "I'm uploading the cosplay video. Thirteen points, here we come!" Alex watched the time-lapse video they'd shot of Cat getting into her costume this morning. Faster than life, she snapped a black-and-purple cape around her neck, quickly freeing her bouncy, blue-tipped curls from under its confines. Alex watched her jump into her loafers, painstakingly hand decorated with comic-book pages. Onto Cat's back, gingerly, went a backpack made entirely of vegetables. Their mom had driven them to the twenty-four-hour grocery at two in the morning to create that monstrosity as stealthily as possible. Their mom was pretty cool, sometimes.

And the video actually looked good. But then, Cat always *did* have a good eye for those kinds of shots.

"Nice one." Alex managed a smile. "Do you have the Hall M passes?"

"*Yes*, I have the Hall M passes, Alex; stop *asking*!" Cat sounded exasperated, probably because Alex had already asked her that same question at least twenty-five times before they'd even reached the con. But he figured it couldn't hurt to check again. The passes were worth their weight in gold, and they'd only gotten them because their parents knew someone who knew someone who owed them a favor. (They were basically impossible to come by.) The passes would allow them to skip the legendarily epic Hall M line. Cat and Alex would've had to get into that line days ago without them. With the passes, they were good to go.

"Okay." Alex shrugged. "Just checking—"

"Holy bananas." Cat cut him off. "Alex, it's them. It's *them*. It's *Team Dangermaker*."

That got Alex to stare out into the crowd. Sure enough, Cat was right (she is that, very occasionally). Standing semi-concealed by a big group of Star-Troopers were Team Dangermaker, the four-person team who'd won the Quest the last three years running. Dahlia, Fox, Rey, and Malik were as close to internet royalty as a person could come without being an actual movie star. They were the very definition of BNFs—Big Name Fans. Everyone wanted to be friends with Team Dangermaker online, but they were notoriously cliquey. Almost no one was good enough to make it to their level of nerd cool and even fewer people had ever seen them IRL. Alex creeped their page with equal amounts of admiration and jealousy. There weren't many photos of them online, but Alex had managed to piece together that they were teens: a girl, a guy, and two enbys (which Alex knew was Dahlia and Fox's way of saying "nonbinary," or someone who fell into their own

15

category outside or somewhere between "boy" and "girl."). But they were the superstars of the Quest world, and looking at the crowd gathered around them, Alex knew that *had* to be Team Dangermaker. Like Cat, he just *knew*. And he and Cat would do their absolute best to dethrone them this year.

. . . But they were still really, really cool.

His family kept moving forward and Alex lost sight of Team Dangermaker. He looked back down at his console. One more escalator and crowded hallway to go. More people he'd have to touch. And then . . . well then, at least, he could focus on the Quest.

3

"I still really can't believe there are this many total and complete nerds in the world," said Fi, stepping on to the escalator and surveying the floor beneath her, packed nearly wall to wall with humans. "Every year I think, *I must have imagined it. It wasn't that many people, was it?* But then I show up here again, and sure enough, somehow it *is* that many people. The people have *multiplied.*"

"Yeah, yeah," Cat said, not bothering to look up from her phone. "We get it. You'd rather be with Ethan and his weird friends."

"*Ethaaaan . . . ,*" Alex teased dreamily, also engrossed in his game.

Fi rolled her eyes because, yeah, they were totally right. Not that Ethan Chaudhuri was her boyfriend or anything, because he wasn't. He *was* the captain of the varsity boys' soccer team, and he *did* have a British accent on account of his fairly recent move to America, and he *also* was on the quiz bowl team, which was nerdy but kind of in an endearing way. He definitely *wasn't* Fi's boyfriend. But he *might* be, if her parents would just let her go on this entirely not-a-big-deal camping weekend that the rest of the cool people in tenth grade were going to.

Well, the entirely-chaperoned-not-a-big-deal camping weekend that she was shocked to have been deemed chill enough to be invited to, considering she was just a ninth grader.

And if she didn't go, that would be *it*. The end. Coolness killer. Deleting-Instagram-level social-status destroyer. Babysitting her nerdcore siblings this weekend was supposed to prove to her parents that she was responsible enough to go, and Fi was willing to put up with the extreme body odor and even-extremer weirdos all weekend if it meant going on that camping trip.

"What would Ethan think of that shirt, anyway?" Cat asked, in a way that would have been innocent if not for that annoying-as-heck little smirk on her face, illuminated by the glow of her phone.

Fi looked down as she stepped off the escalator, panicking all over again about the coffee-stained leopard-print blouse she had literally taken off her mother's back to save her a day of extreme embarrassment. She looked like a hundred-year-old mom who didn't know how to hold a travel mug. It was her least cute look of all time, a world away from her big, soft tees. She didn't throw this term around lightly, but Fi was basically a hero, thank you very much. More of a superhero than any of the costumed nerds at this con.

Still, it was certainly not the epitome of cool she was hoping for today—and would definitely not be ending up on social media (unless it was, like, artfully shot from the collarbone up, or she stooped to using that extremely nerdcore con filter to cover it up).

"At least I'm not wearing those shoes," Fi shot back. The only part of Cat's outfit that wasn't all costumey were a pair of loafers that she'd stuck comic-book pages all over with craft glue. Incredibly uncute.

"They're a Quest item." Cat waved her off. "And thank you for reminding me to upload a pic of them; that's nineteen whole points."

"Are you even still getting signal in here?" Fi looked quizzically at Cat's phone.

"I better keep getting signal," Cat replied, hurrying to catch up with their parents and Julie. "The Quest updates all day, and we have to stay on top of it."

"The Quest?" Fi asked, rushing behind her.

Cat looked back with that look Fi hated, the one where Cat obviously thought that she was the smartest person in the whole world. "The Quest, Fi. *The Quest*. We've talked about it for weeks? Do you ever pay attention to me when I talk?"

Okay, so maybe Fi didn't *always* pay attention when Cat talked.

Their gang had to turn around and annoy everyone in the hallway behind them by quickly flipping directions—Julie had just realized they'd been walking the wrong way. Cat sighed. "*The Quest*. The biggest scavenger hunt in the world? Run by *Paranormal*'s Corwin Blake?"

Fi blinked in a way that she hoped conveyed just how little she knew or cared about any of this. It did not, unfortunately, deter her younger sister, who threw her arms in the air in frustration.

"Corwin Blake?! Hottest actor in maybe the entire world? Plays a deeply troubled and lovingly rumpled ghost on *Paranormal*? The show about the ghost-hunting brothers? Which has been running for eleven seasons? And the one brother is probably in love with the ghost even though they'll never say it?"

Fi shrugged. "What does this have to do with your scavenging?"

"Agh!" Cat was *really* laying it on thick now. "Corwin Blake runs the world's biggest scavenger hunt every year at this con. Without Geeki-Con's permission, but still. All the items on the Quest list are posted online right before the convention, you can only compete in teams of up to four people, and you upload pictures and videos of all your completed items to the Quest app." Cat waved her phone in Fi's face.

Fi batted it away. "But *why*, though?"

"Because." Cat sighed. "The people who complete the most items and win the Quest get to hang with Corwin and his *Paranormal* costars for a *week* doing charity work, building houses for families in need."

"And," Alex interjected, surprising his sisters, "there are potential mentorships on the line with the TV show's crew. Your career . . . or your art, for example," he added, conspicuously casually, "could get a real boost."

"And that." Cat nodded aggressively. "And also it really can't be stressed enough that we really absolutely must win it at all costs this year or else what is even the *point of anything ever anymore—*"

"*Okay*, whoa," Fi interrupted her younger sister. "Got it. So this little game is, like, your whole thing this weekend?"

"It's *our* whole thing *today*," said Alex as they all finally came to a stop in front of what Fi assumed must be their parents' panel room. "It's one day only. And *you* can do whatever you want."

"Right," Fi said under her breath as they all filed into the room, grabbing a few of the reserved seats near the front as their parents rushed onto the stage. "I wish."

4

Cat's foot bobbed up and down against the concrete floor. Her parents' panel had started late, and *as predicted*, it was absolutely, positively going to go over the allotted time. Her parents had spent the last hour dodging questions about the reboot they were obviously (but secretly) working on, and now the Q and A had turned into people pretending they were going to ask a question but really talking about themselves. The *worst*.

"This is never going to *end*," Cat groaned to Alex. He was seated next to her, just a few rows from the front of the room. The folding chairs were hard and uncomfortable, as usual. Cat just wanted to get on with the Quest and their next list item, and they were *stuck here*. It was so frustrating!

Alex just shrugged. "Why don't you look over the Quest list again? We can never be too prepared. Do you have the Hall M passes?"

"*Yes*, Alex, again, *yes*." Cat jiggled her knee harder. "Okay. Yeah. Good idea."

She pulled out her phone—signal still strong. Thank the glorious goddess of GeekiCon. She opened the Quest app and waited for the list to load up. And there it was.

Corwin Blake was known for being kind of an eclectic oddball—a super-handsome dark-eyed scruffy-haired eclectic oddball with a wide, goofy smile and flawless deep brown skin and just the right amount of beardy stubble in the same deep shade as his messy curls and with a following in the millions, but still. He'd helped so many people by doing the Quest—each participant paid a small entry fee that went to charity, and winning the grand prize meant hanging with Corwin and his friends for a week building houses for under-privileged families.

Cat shoved daydreams of home building with Corwin to the back of her mind and refocused on the list in front of her, leg still bouncing.

The Quest

1. A time-lapse video of your team getting into cosplay for the convention. (13 points) *Done!! Hopefully it makes the full thirteen points...*

2. A photo of yourself with the WELCOME TO GEEKICON banner. (11 points) *SO done.*

3. Create the ultimate con backpack... out of vegetables. (20 points) *Done.*

4. Decoupage your con shoes with pages from your favorite (... or least favorite) comic book. (19 points) *Done and stylin'; shut up, Fi.*

5. Find the Quest donation box and drop off a toy from the convention floor. (56 points)

6. Volunteer to help at an Artist Alley booth that is definitely not yours. (35 points)

7. Get a voice actor to record a dramatic retelling of your Quest adventure. (54 points)

8. Cartwheel down the center aisle in Hall M. (100 points) *SOON*

DUE BY

the end of

Geeki CON

Day 1!

THE QUEST CONTINUES!

9. Convince three *Vigilante League* cosplayers to sing "Eye of the Tiger" with you. (37 points)

10. Give a flower to a con volunteer. (46 points)

11. Write a poem for someone you see on the con floor who looks like they could use a pick-me-up. Give it to them! (24 points)

12. Bring heroes together. Have a tea party with Lady Lynx, Dark Spider, and the Cowl. (16 points)

13. Collect the contact information of three new friends. (18 points)

14. Give up your spot in line to someone who needs it more than you do. (62 points)

15. Beat someone at *Hexforce Legends* on the convention floor. Create and capture your own victory dance. (22 points)

16. Get a real-life comic-book artist to sign your team name in their own comic. (76 points)

17. Sneak up on one of your fellow team members and videotape the jump scare. (14 points)

18. Play a sport on the main escalators. (20 points)

19. Find cosplayers in enough colors to make a double rainbow. (29 points)

20. You believe you can fly. (25 points) *What does this even mean?*

21. How many people can you get to sing your favorite TV show theme song at once? (39 points)

22. Even baddies have to stay in shape. Participate in Dancercize with a Star-Trooper squad. (44 points)

23. High-five another Quest team. How high can you go, actually? (30 points)

24. Ask a question at a panel without making it about yourself. (12 points) *About to happen. Ducky McFowl, suckers!*

FIND MORE **CHALLENGES** ON THE NEXT PAGE!

25. Pass a hat around a crowded panel and collect donations for charity. The panelists must sing until the hat has reached every person in the room. (83 points)

26. Submit a photo of the most beautiful thing at GeekiCon. (45 points)

27. Create a portrait of your favorite convention guest out of the medium of your choice, and give it to them. Traditional art materials disallowed. (40 points)

28. Convince a cosplayer dressed as a character you've never heard of that you definitely know who they are. (24 points)

29. Share a photo of your team eating healthy at the convention! Maybe the most challenging item of all! (46 points)

30. Discover if aliens are ticklish. (With their permission only!) (16 points)

31. Post about your new favorite artist from Artist Alley on your social media. (31 points)

32. Take a photo with your biggest fan. (18 points)

Cat closed the app with a sigh—it seemed like *so much*. Every item looked so simple at first glance, and yet the more she thought each of them through, the more they seemed to grow horns and tails and swing at the twins with the ferocity of a monster on a particularly bad night. How did Team Dangermaker manage to win three years in a row? How did they always manage to complete every item?

To win, you had to complete as many items as possible to get the highest score. *Plus*, certain people who impressed Corwin and the judges the most even qualified to be considered for special mentorships—Alex cared way more about those. Not only did you have to complete as many items as possible to receive points—awarded by a super-secret Quest judging committee—but you were also awarded extra points for style. Taking a photo with your biggest fan was fine, but taking a photo with a ceiling fan the size of a football field somehow would definitely net a team the full eighteen points. There was a lot of creativity and on-the-spot thinking involved. It definitely wasn't easy. And the team with the most points won.

And the Q and A was somehow *still going*, with yet another "this is more of a comment than a question, but . . ." from the crowd. In desperation, Cat threw her hand up in the air. Her mom, spotting it immediately, laughed and waved for Cat to stand up. "Everyone, my daughter, Catalina," she said in her characteristic accent.

"Um, hi, everybody." Cat stood up, holding her phone out in front of her in selfie video mode. She could feel Fi's eyes boring a hole into the side of her head, but whatever. "I wanted to ask, like, an actual question, actually. Can you talk a little bit about what it was like moving from writing comics scripts to writing TV scripts? Like, what the difference is?" She sat back down with a hard *thud* and started jiggling her knee again. She hit stop on the video with a smile.

Fi reached over Alex and pressed the palm of her hand into Cat's bobbing knee. "Can you not?" she said, glaring at Cat. No, Cat could not *not*. She just needed to get out of here, stat. They really did have to get to their next Quest item and soon. Plus, there was a special, exclusive screening of her most favorite cartoon of all time, *Igor!!! on Skates*, an anime about a boy figure skater who falls in love with one of his boy figure skater friends. They were showing a brand-new episode in just ten minutes, which wouldn't have been a problem if her parents' panel had ended ten minutes ago like it was supposed to! Plus, obviously they were missing out on precious time for completing Quest items elsewhere. This was a total and complete nightmare.

But an attitude wouldn't get Cat anywhere with Fi, who was going through a moody phase and could out-attitude anyone in her sleep. Cat needed her big sister on her side. "Fi," she whispered, learning over, "can we just—?"

"*Shhh!*" Fi hissed, and a man in wolf ears directly in front of them spun around, shushing her right back. Fi shrank back and Cat smiled to herself. *Served her right*, thought Cat. Fi had been *way* louder than she'd been.

Turning back toward the raised stage, Cat pulled at a strand of her curly hair, currently blue tipped, her foot still bobbing. Alex was sitting between his sisters and, of course, didn't look concerned at all. He probably hadn't even noticed the time; he had moved from his console to his sketchbook. Cat knew sometimes it was the only way Alex could keep calm. But she needed someone to complain to. Cat reached out to grab his pencil.

"Hey!" Alex wrenched his pencil back from his sister's grasp. Wolf Ears spun around in his chair again to glare at him. There was no way they were escaping without this guy complaining to their parents after the panel. *Ugh*.

Cat thought fast. "It's twenty after!" she whispered, jabbing a finger at Alex's calculator watch. "We're never going to make it. We're getting foiled by this panel."

They were *completely* almost late now. Would they be stuck here until the bitter end? Cat let out an even louder sigh and sunk back into her seat. Alex was never the take-action guy. That was all going to be on Cat, which she was fine with—it meant she got to do things the way she wanted them done.

But still. It would have been nice to have some help.

Cat felt weighted down, like she might slide off her chair and melt directly into the floor. At least then she'd be able to ooze her way across the patterned carpet, out the door, into the hallway, and on to her freedom. The Quest awaited!

Cat shook her head and pulled herself upright. Now was not the time for daydreaming. Now was the time for *decisions*. If there was anything anime had taught her, it was that sitting around and waiting for things to happen to you was absolutely not the way to get stuff done. No, actually, that was how you invited giant, terrifying titans into your city to eat you and everyone you love.

Not today, titans. *Not today.*

It was time to make things happen. As casually as humanly possible, Cat peered over Alex's head to sneak a glance at Fi. She seemed engrossed in the never-ending panel, but a second look showed Cat that her sister was *actually* staring hard at a guy farther down the reserved row—totally her type (messy curls, disinterested stare)—and compulsively tucking and untucking her flat-ironed hair behind her ear. Cat almost rolled her eyes before she realized that this particular Teenage Moment™ had provided her with the perfect momentary distraction. It was now or never. Cat got Alex's attention and jerked her head toward the aisle.

Checking one more time to make sure Fi wasn't looking her way, Cat grabbed hold of her cape, ducked, and slipped right out of her aisle seat. *Success!* Crouching and praying to as many magical girls as she could think of, Cat imagined some epic movie score playing as she made the bid for her escape. Half-bent as she ran, Cat arrived at the back of the room and stood up straight, nodding at the girl with braces in a lime-green con T-shirt staffing the door. The girl narrowed her eyes and pushed the door open just an inch.

But an inch was all Cat and Alex would need. That was their out. They'd almost made it. Cat took a step toward the door before freezing dead in her tracks, the back of her neck prickling with a really bad feeling. She turned slowly.

Her brother wasn't behind her.

Alex.

She couldn't just leave him here to suffer. They were in this together. It was dangerous to go alone. Cat stood on her tiptoes at the back of the room to try to get a good look at her brother near the front, crossing her fingers that Fi didn't choose this moment to turn around. She quickly pulled her phone out of her circular Alora Florals purse and swiped until she found Alex's name in her text message list.

Cattails: You were supposed to follow me!

Alex, trying to be as casual as possible, brought his phone to his face and quickly typed something. Cat felt her phone buzz.

Alinator: go without me

Alinator: save yourself

Cat bit her lip, smearing some of her blue lipstick in the process. It was tempting. Freedom, and their next Quest items, and *Igor*, were so close. But if she left Alex here, they wouldn't be *their* Quest items. They would be hers.

Cat sighed. Sometimes Alex would freeze up, and it was up to Cat to get him to move. She really didn't want to resort to this, but there was no way around it. Pulling up the GIF keyboard on her phone, Cat sent Alex one thing: a looping video of their two favorite *Wormhole* characters grabbing hands and running through alien chaos.

From the back of the room, Cat could see her brother's head pop up to look for her. He twisted all the way around in his chair and caught Cat's eye—which was enough to gain Fi's attention, too.

Her older sister bolted up and out of her seat so fast it was like she had a jet pack on her butt.

Cat knew she had to act fast. She lunged past the lime-shirted volunteer, slamming the double doors of the panel room open all the way. Before the crowd in the room could turn to fully see what was going on, Cat ducked down behind the last row of seats and yelled as loud as she possibly could: "Listen, I just think the prequels are better movies than the original *Star Worlds* trilogy!"

The room exploded. The panelists, Cat's parents included, sat in shock as the crowd of *Ducky McFowl* fans turned to see who had caused the disruption. But Cat knew people loved arguing about (sorry, "having a spirited debate" about) *Star Worlds*, and in no time the crowd had devolved into a massive group argument.

As the panelists tried to regain some order over the crowd, Cat ran the length of the aisle she had snuck down before and grabbed her brother's hand from behind. Cat pulled Alex away just as Fi made a grab for them. Instead of heading into the crush of people, Cat bolted to the curtain that acted as a makeshift backstage area for the panelists and flew through it, dragging Alex behind her.

"Cat?!" Alex shook his hand free from hers but kept pace with his sister.

She turned a corner, slammed through a set of double doors at breakneck speed, and skidded to a stop near an alcove. Alex almost ran straight into her back.

"Watch it!" she whispered, dragging Alex back into the shadows.

Cat took stock of where they'd ended up. Instead of running into the main hall, she'd taken them backstage into the brightly lit corridors and

service tunnels that served the convention center, the ones the very stars themselves used to
get around during con weekends without being
mobbed.

Totally on purpose, Cat thought. *Completely
planned out. Yup.*

While Alex put his hands on his knees and
tried to regain his breath, Cat attempted to figure
out how far they'd run.

"This was a terrible idea," heaved Alex.

Ignoring him, Cat counted the doors behind
her—one, two, three . . . wait.

Wait.

"This way," Cat insisted. Passing a wall of
catering dishes, a cageful of golf carts, and what
looked like a weird open garage, they came to a
halt in front of another door identical to the one
from which they'd escaped.

"Don't. Say. A word," Cat whispered to her
brother.

"You're the one who can't stop talking," Alex
whispered back as Cat slowly pushed the door
open.

Slipping through, Alex just a step after her,
Cat silently closed the door behind them. They
were in a dark room behind another set of curtains, next to a giant stage. There was no one on

this side of the backstage area, but through the semi-sheer curtains Cat could see a crowd of hundreds seated in uncomfortable chairs, staring toward the stage.

"Holy Danica McKellar, Cat," Alex breathed. "We did it."

Slowly, Cat turned. There, projected up on the screen onstage: the *Igor!!! on Skates* opening credits.

They'd made it.

Trying to stay chill and quiet and failing miserably, Cat hopped around in joy and got Alex to join in, too. They had barely missed a second of the episode! And they'd lost Fi in the process! It was a GeekiCon miracle.

Cat and Alex sat on the carpeted floor behind the stage with a prime view of the whole new episode from the sidelines. Cat's love for this show was so deep. Igor had these amazing roller-skating dancing moves *and* a cute boyfriend! There was nothing better in life.

Cat was so caught up in the episode that she almost forgot the *other* reason they'd had to make a break for it: the Quest. Hurriedly, she whipped out her phone and uploaded the video she'd taken of herself asking an actually good question at her parents' panel to the app. Another one down.

"Hey!" a sharp voice whispered from behind them. "What are you doing back here?"

Cat turned sharply and scrambled up off the floor. A guy wearing a suit jacket over a nerdy T-shirt and holding a mic loomed over her, his arms crossed over his chest. He was a middle-aged white dude, and his bright CON STAFF badge told Cat his name was JAMES M. His eyes locked on to Cat's phone.

"We're just—"

"Are you one of those *Questers*?" James M. demanded, pointing at Cat's phone. "There are no scavenger hunts permitted on con premises and anyone caught participating will be immediately removed from the convention!"

Oh, yeah, Cat remembered. The Quest was *definitely* not endorsed by GeekiCon. Alex was frozen solid, of course, and would be no help here, naturally.

"We're with the panelists." Cat tucked her phone behind her back and pulled out the excuse she always used backstage at her parents' events. "What are *you* doing back here?" she countered, a lot more boldly than she felt.

"I'm moderating the next panel. What kind of pass is that?" the guy asked, reaching out to grab the credentials around her neck—the ones that *absolutely* did not qualify her to be backstage at the *Igor!!! on Skates* panel.

"Uh, see, here's the thing—" Alex began.

It was a big deal for Alex to speak up, and Cat tried to think up her next lie quickly. She opened her mouth—but was cut off by a sudden commotion in the crowd.

"It's a Mewblue!" Cat heard someone shriek. Through the sheers, she could see a woman stand up with her phone held aloft, an AR game active on the screen, the one where you captured tiny animalesque creatures for fun. "Mewblue onstage! Right now!"

James M.'s head spun, distracted momentarily by the crowd, and Cat knew this was another make-or-break moment.

They'd seen the *Igor!!! on Skates* episode, they'd checked off another Quest item—how many other challenges could they complete today? Was there still time to get in line for the limited-edition *Dwarves & Drama* figure? Could they try to sneak into the *Voltage: Defenders of Legend* panel? Only one way to find out—and that was to *move*.

Cat pushed Alex toward the curtains. She didn't trust him to follow this time.

"Wait!" She could hear James M.'s angry voice behind her, but she didn't stop—and didn't let Alex stop, either. Together they dove into the massive crowd that had surged toward the stage with phones held aloft. The twins disappeared, anonymous in the nerdy masses.

24. Ask a question at a panel without making it about yourself. (12 points)

5

"I can't believe we haven't run into Fi yet."

Alex's eyes darted away from an awesome piece of *Whom, M.D.* fan art at a table in Artist Alley. He was so sure his older sister was going to pop up right behind the artist's booth and give him that look he hated. It was going to happen. It *had* to. He was going to be in so much trouble, and he would never be able to ask his parents to get him that *Whom* print and they were never going to get to come to GeekiCon again and they *definitely* were never going to win the Quest and—

"Relax," Cat coaxed behind him. Alex turned quickly, shaken out of his thoughts, to see her holding up a pair of earrings next to her face. "What do you think of these?"

Alex shook his head. How could Cat concentrate on accessorizing at a time like this? Still, he turned back and took a business card from that *Whom, M.D.* artist anyway. She was really, really good at drawing his favorite M.D., and he wanted to remember to come back to her, even if he wasn't able to concentrate on anything else today.

"Okay," Alex said to his sister, looking down at his watch. Nearly noon already. "The *Epic* signing is soon. If we want to make it, we need to start moving now." Cat sighed, but Alex knew that *she* knew that he was right. It was absolute chaos on the floor, a crowd that was going to take the two of them a while to maneuver, let alone getting into line and hoping that they hadn't arrived too late. *Epic* was Alex's favorite comic book in the entire world. The artist on it, Adrianna Tack, blew him away every month with the way she lovingly rendered the heroic space opera. Alex couldn't miss this signing.

"So where to, O wise one?" Cat asked in mock seriousness. She put the earrings back down on the table, thanked the artist, and linked elbows with Alex.

Alex looked down at their linked arms for a moment before accepting that this was a thing that was happening. He popped out his phone to check the map on the GeekiCon app. "Looks like . . . Pixel Comics, booth 2729."

Cat's eyes got wide. "All the way past the gigantic AC Comics setup?"

"No, right before it," Alex clarified. "What number is their autograph on the Quest list?"

Cat whipped out her phone again. "Shoot, already low battery. It's . . . 'Get a real-life comic-book artist to sign your team name in their own comic.' Item sixteen. Seventy-six points! This might put us in the running with Team Danger-maker!"

Alex nodded firmly. Good thing they picked a respectable team name. Team DoubleTrouble. Because they were twins. And because it kind of felt like Dangermaker, in a way.

They could do this. *He* could do this.

"We got this!" he said uncharacteristically, and momentarily filled with the confidence and excitement you get from being surrounded by all of your favorite things, bright colors, and even brighter lights.

But as Alex stepped from Artist Alley into the main aisle beside it, he suddenly found himself moving way faster than he thought he would be. Way, *way* faster.

"*Caaaaaat!*" he yelled, his arm slipping through hers. "We don't got this! *We don't got this!*"

Was this what it felt like to be trapped in your worst nightmare? Because this might just be Alex's worst nightmare. He'd had a lot of nightmares, and this was definitely, absolutely one of them.

All around Alex, completely surrounding him, were swarms of the undead. Pushed along by a mass of rotting arms and limping legs, all Alex could see and hear were flashes of blood dripping from gaping mouths and the constant, unending stream of "*Rrraaaaghhhh!!*" coming from every side. His vision was filled with reds and browns, grime and guts. Too many strangers, too close . . .

This is the zombie apocalypse, thought Alex. *This is how I go.*

Alex knew about fight or flight. He'd read all about it and the chemicals that flooded your brain. Were they flooding his right now? Channeling the power of ten thousand lens flares, Alex disentangled himself from the shuffling limbs and shot sideways, flattening himself against the nearest booth. He let the horde pass him by. A zombie stampede. In the middle of the con floor. You never knew what you were going to find at GeekiCon. Which is why Alex both loved and hated it in equal measure at all times.

"Cat!" yelled Alex, flailing his arms as high as he could reach, trying to peer above the crowd. "Cat, where are you?!" Catching the disapproving stare of one of the booth workers, Alex dropped his hands and turned red, reaching for his phone instead.

Alex: almost became one of the walking dead

Cat: lol me too

Alex: by the booth with all the big fancy statues
Alex: come find me

Alex put his phone away, hopeful that Cat would find him in time. There were so many people on the floor, half of them in incredible but extremely large costumes. He hated getting separated from Cat even for a moment—it was always nearly impossible to find each other again. Plus, they were almost late for the signing, but at least he was guaranteed a spot if he made it in time—his parents had made sure he had a wristband.

Wait. Alex suddenly felt something was wrong—a disturbance in the con. He turned to see a sign held aloft in the distance by some volunteer.

EPIC SIGNING—LINE CAPPED.

Line capped.

Line capped?!

The Epic *signing was full, and his life was utterly and completely over.*

"No, no, no," Alex whispered to himself. The one Quest item he'd told Cat he could handle, and it had literally slipped from his very hands. This wasn't going according to plan. Alex liked things when they went according to plan. He liked when things felt *right*. When things felt wrong, it was almost like he had a full-body itch that he couldn't scratch. He got that wrong feeling occasionally; like when he saw a cosplay that wasn't quite accurate (itch), or when someone quoted a line from *Wormhole* incorrectly (double itch), or when plans didn't work out (triple mega-itch!). And now he was one big itch, *and* he'd lost the chance to meet Adrianna Tack . . .

"What?" asked a far-too-cheerful voice from beside him. Alex was too caught up in his dread over missing the signing to feel grateful that Cat had finally managed to find him on the floor.

"Check it out." Cat held her phone out proudly. "I crowd surfed the zombie horde! Somebody managed to snap a pic. That's *totally for sure* going to count for those twenty-five 'I believe I can fly' points—I definitely *felt* like I was flying—"

Why wouldn't she stop talking?! Didn't Cat understand how important this was?

"Cat," Alex interrupted her, frustrated. "The line for *Epic*, for the signing," he said quickly, running his hands through his hair. "It's closed. *Closed!*"

Cat blinked. "How?!"

"The—the zombies," Alex stuttered, frantically looking at the floor in their area. "We're never going to meet Adrianna Tack. Never! We'll be a Quest item down with no way to fix it, and it's all my—"

"Stop. It's okay," Cat said, but Alex could hear in her voice that she was trying to convince herself as much as she was him. "Take deep breaths like Dad says. It's okay."

When Alex was spinning out into everything he was worried about and felt like he couldn't breathe, his parents told him to just take deep breaths. It was so hard to remember to do unless someone told him to. Alex nodded at Cat and dropped to the floor, crossing his legs. He had to keep busy and keep feeling like he was making progress in the right direction and, and . . .

"I'm being serious, Alex—stop and breathe." She squatted next to him so they were facing each other.

Alex concentrated on Cat's face and nothing else, his eyes wide. He breathed in as Cat counted to five and breathed out on the next count of five.

Cat smiled as Alex breathed. "I'm going to get us that autograph."

Alex's heart rate was dropping; his vision was coming back into focus. "How?"

"This is GeekiCon," Cat said, pushing herself up to stand. She held out her hand for Alex to take. "This is where magic happens."

Alex felt a little less shaky. He took Cat's hand with a nod and stood up. "Do you still have the Hall M passes?"

"*Yes*," Cat insisted. On seeing Alex's skeptical look, she added, "Don't worry. I checked."

He nodded and followed his sister as she marched toward the Pixel booth, dodging a stroller and a massive pair of brown, feathered wings on a cosplayer in the process.

In what felt like no time, distracted by the

colorful cosplay all around him, Alex suddenly found himself nearly colliding with his sister's back once again.

"That *keeps* happening . . ." Alex rubbed at his forehead.

"Well . . . ," Cat said, looking back at him. "We've made it."

Alex looked up at the lime-clad volunteer next to them and the END OF LINE sign she had in her hand. "This is the end of the line," the volunteer drawled.

Alex stared straight ahead. He had no idea what to do.

". . . But there's another signing at three o'clock today."

Alex turned to look at the volunteer so slowly he felt like he was in an action movie. "There is?"

The volunteer looked at him strangely. (People did that a lot.) "Yeah. Just get here earlier for that one. You know this is GeekiCon, right?"

Alex laughed a laugh that didn't sound at all like him, pure relief escaping from his mouth in gasps. "Oh! Right! Sure!"

Cat smiled at him and reached out for Alex's hand. Alex looked down and grabbed it. "Three o'clock," Cat repeated. "We'll see you then."

"Whatever." The volunteer waved them off.

Alex couldn't believe it. GeekiCon had blessed them. He had seen victory slip from his grasp, only to have it reappear in front of him. At three o'clock. It was the luckiest thing that had ever happened to him. It was—

"Oh no," whispered Cat, tugging on Alex's hand, hard, and interrupting his thoughts.

"What?" Alex asked, concerned. That wasn't a good sign. That was never a good sign.

"Fi," was all Cat said—and all she needed to say. Alex spun around and saw their older sister's face hovering above the crowd. She must have been on her tiptoes, searching for them.

Seeing Fi's face brought Alex swiftly and painfully back to the real world. They were in serious trouble if she found them, and they still had a ton of items to get through. Fi had that expression on her face she always got when she was angry, the one with the raised eyebrow and the weird thing with her lip. Yep, there was no doubt in Alex's mind—it was time to run.

But not before he checked on his *Epic* comic, ensuring its safety inside its bag and board in his messenger bag. He had his priorities, after all.

20. You believe you can fly.
(25 points)

6

"I am *not* going back to eating lunch in the library alone because of a *comics convention*," Fi said to no one in particular, turning in circles in the middle of the show floor. It was hopeless. There were tens of thousands of dang nerds in this building. What chance did she have of finding two wayward twelve-year-olds? None. Absolutely none. She was toast. The toastiest. Burned toast. Burned toast who eats lunch in the library with no friends like the dork she really was.

It was a miracle that she'd managed to run out of the *Ducky McFowl* panel before her mom and dad noticed that she'd lost the twins anyway. She'd been avoiding her parents' texts ever since, scrolling frantically through GeekiCon's tag on social media, before remembering the name of that stupid scavenger hunt her sister had been babbling about earlier. She'd searched #thequest in a panic, desperately seeking any sign of her siblings.

And she found them—not that it did her any good. It seemed like every five seconds one or both of those little nerdy nightmares were updating their story: Cat and Alex in the middle of a rainbow of cosplayers, twenty-nine points! Cat and Alex having a tea party with some dude with giant gold horns, a lady in a black catsuit, and something called the Cowl, sixteen points! A video of some voice actor saying the twins' team name into Cat's camera and wishing them luck, fifty-four points! (Well, close enough to earn them *some* points, anyway.) It was impossible to keep up with the two of them, and there was no telling where they'd be headed next.

As Fi kept scrolling, she almost started to envy the odd little world the two of them shared. How did all these different weirdos come together to admire the things they loved in a space like this? How did twins so different end up enjoying such similar things?

She shook her head. *Nah.* She would rather be her own independent person than be half of a constant pair or just another face in the crowd. As long as she, as her own independent person, wore the right clothes and had the right friends and got to go on a chaperoned and not-a-big-deal-at-all camping trip with the right boy in three weeks, of course.

Turning slowly in a circle, ignoring the annoyed glances from passersby, Fi *thought* she recalled something about a comic book that Alex was obsessed with—but she wouldn't even know where to start looking for something like that. Why hadn't she paid more attention to those nerds when they'd talked about their nerd stuff? Every inch of the floor was jammed with cosplay-ers and fans and volunteers and *why did the twins have to be so darn short and also wily?!* This would never happen at one of her soccer games. Why couldn't her siblings just have been like . . . easier to understand and enjoyed good old-fashioned soccer? Instead, she was stuck here playing social media stalker with their Instagram accounts. And no one cool from Instagram was even *at* this ridiculous convention. *Also,* Fi thought to herself in the final throes of despair:

Everything.

Smells.

Terrible!

Worse than the worst locker room. Worse than her gym bag. The combination of sweaty nerds packed together in a tight space, many drenched with extreme amounts of body spray, and what must have been a combination of plastic from the booths and pizza from the only food stalls in the hall, was absolutely and entirely overwhelming.

Letting loose a frustrated scream for which she only got a couple of strange looks (what even *was* this place?! Was screaming a normal thing here?!), Fi stormed toward the floor exit with a ferocity in her eyes that dared anyone to get in her way. She could be on the field right now, getting in a practice before the next game of the season. But *nooo*, instead she was on *Adventures in Babysitting* duty at the world's largest geek show. And if she saw another bat-carrying clown girl, she was going to *explode*.

Fi slammed through the doors into the breezeway, slapping her pass against the exit scanner so abruptly that she almost knocked over the volunteer staffing it. Finally—*finally*—Fi found herself outside in the scorching midday heat. Fi didn't care how humid or sweaty she got now—she could finally breathe again. Why did all these people want to spend a beautiful day like today trapped inside with a bunch of sweaty dweebs?

She had never felt like such an outsider in all her life—though, admittedly, that was by design. If she thought about it too hard, she could almost be impressed by the sheer no-cares-given attitude of most of the people in this crowd. Had she ever been so unapologetically *herself*? Fi wondered. She turned her face up toward the sun and just stood there for a moment, sucking in a deep breath . . .

. . . Right. The *twins*.

Fi sighed. Never an uninteresting moment. Time to find them so she could lose 'em—for a week of camping with people who *mattered*.

7. Get a voice actor to record a dramatic retelling of your Quest adventure. (54 points)

12. Bring heroes together. Have a tea party with Lady Lynx, Dark Spider, and the Cowl. (16 points)

19. Find cosplayers in enough colors to make a double rainbow. (29 points)

7

Cat's feet hurt and her back hurt and her eyes even hurt a little from staring at everything for so long, but honestly she'd also never felt better. She and Alex had managed to avoid Fi all morning, they had a plan in place to get Alex his *Epic* signature, and they were checking things off the Quest list like it was their homework assignment. GeekiCon? More like Crushed-It Con!

Alex would totally hate that. Which is why Cat kept it to herself. At least *she* thought she was hilarious.

Cat glanced back at Alex. He was sitting cross-legged on the floor again, flipping through pages of his sketchbook. The twins were safely hidden in a massive line for the *Hexforce Legends* VR challenge, having snuck in right as they were opening a new window for players. They'd only have to wait a few more minutes until they reached the front of the line, when they'd step up to one of thirty game stations and pop on a VR headset. Winning a *Hexforce Legends* match on the con floor was one of the more difficult Quest items, but Cat wasn't worried; she'd been watching streamers play every day online for weeks before the con. She knew all the tricks. She was prepped. She was so totally ready.

"You know, like, a thousand people will have worn these headsets on their faces before us, right?" asked Alex, still not looking up from his sketchbook. "We're probably going to catch lice. Or some weird rash."

"Chill." Cat waved him off. "That doesn't happen." She considered for a moment. "It probably doesn't happen. I'm sure it definitely doesn't happen. You just don't want to play."

"You're right," agreed Alex, closing his sketchbook. "VR makes my head hurt. It's not made for people who already wear glasses."

"You're fine at 3-D movies."

"I *hate* 3-D movies."

"Okay, fair," Cat conceded reluctantly. "Listen,

it's totally fine if you don't want to play. I can handle this on my own. I've watched Normageddon play for over a hundred hours. I'm basically a master."

"You've literally played this game three times before today," Alex clarified.

First of all, how dare he. "Just you wait, Alessandro Gallo." Cat stood up tall, spinning on one of her decoupaged feet. Her cape smacked the person in front of her in line, and she had to quickly apologize, yanking it back. "Oops. All I'm saying is"—Cat spread her arms wide in a victory pose—"I'm going to crush it."

Alex just stared at her. "Cool." He did not sound convinced.

Whatever, thought Cat determinedly. *I've got this.*

"Next in line, let's go, let's go," a lime-shirted volunteer drawled, waving the next fifty in line forward to their stations. This was them! They were up!

"Let's go, let's go!" Cat repeated, hurriedly helping Alex to his feet and rushing over to the nearest open station. Alex took his spot next to her, carefully tucking his sketchbook back into his messenger bag.

Cat grabbed the headset from the small station

in front of her—okay, yeah, there were definitely a million other people's germs on here, but oh well—and slid it over her mass of curls. She took a peek at Alex next to her—he was doing the same thing. Good for him. *Face your fears!* Cat thought with an inner fist pump. She grabbed her mask with both hands and snapped it down over her eyes, the headphones coming to rest on her ears.

All at once, GeekiCon disappeared. Okay, it still smelled like GeekiCon for sure. But Cat could almost forget that. She'd been transported to an entirely different world. She was flying in a ship over a colorful desertscape, the ground passing by beneath her with alarming speed. Cat checked her team makeup—Alex and three random con-goers who had the stations next to them.

They could do this. *They could do this.*

Cat made the call to jump, and in first-person POV, she and her team of five leaped from the ship, launching themselves toward the ground with dizzying speed.

"*Woooo!*" Cat yelled as she soared through the air, before snapping her mouth shut. She'd forgotten there was probably a crowd of people watching her, seeing whatever she saw projected on a flat-screen above her station. *Be cool, Cat. Be cool.*

Cat's avatar landed on the desert ground with

a loud *thud*. As she started the wild scramble to find a weapon, she saw Alex's character doing the same. He was doing such a great job despite his motion sickness. She was so happy for him, giving it a real go like this!

Cat shook her head. She was getting distracted and still had no weapon to speak of. As Cat opened barrel after barrel, she found nothing but health packs and weapon mods. But as she turned to run toward another building, she saw something flashy out of the corner of her eye on the ground. Someone else must have dropped their weapon! Waving her arms around IRL (she must look ridiculous but totally didn't care), Cat scooped up the rainbow-tinted weapon and her avatar equipped it. Finally. She was ready. It was time . . .

. . . to *hide*.

Yep, that was her big, fancy tactic. Hide until everyone else had killed one another and then come out swinging in the final moments to deal a devastating blow to the other team. She'd watched the famous streamer Normageddon do it to great success a million times before. Some people might call it a dirty trick, but Cat didn't care. Cat called it *how to be a dang winner*. Plus, only people who weren't in the game could see what she was doing on the flat-screen over her head. Everyone she was actually competing against was safely ensconced in the world of the game. She had nothing to worry about.

Cat ran into the nearest building and crouched in a corner. She saw Alex burst into the small wooden shack and find his own corner to camp in. Their teammates, the random guys (*or girls! Or neither! Don't be accidentally gender normative, Cat, jeez*), stood in the room just looking at them.

"Are we going, or what?" said one of the randoms over voice chat.

"We're staying right here," said Cat with far more confidence than she felt.

The other player paused. "Yeah, okay. I can get into that." The other three players tucked themselves into the room's remaining corners.

And time started to tick by. Ten other squads left. Then eight. Now seven. They had to quickly jet from shack to metal bunker to slightly larger shack to stay inside the ever-shrinking area of play. But they'd managed to successfully avoid seeing another person's avatar for pushing thirteen whole minutes now. By Cat's standards, this was a great success.

"We're doing great!" Cat encouraged over voice chat. They'd slowly increased the quality of their weapons and gear over time, and they were looking truly poised to be winners.

"So long as we don't choke the second we see another team," said one of their randoms dryly.

"We won't," Alex piped up from beside Cat. She grinned. That was the spirit!

The area of play shrank one last time and their team made a run for it. Safely inside the big metal walls of a bunker, they settled in. Cat watched the team counter tick down to five teams. Four teams. Now three. And then . . . just one other team was left standing.

"This is it—" Cat was cut off by the sudden sounds of footsteps. She swung around, her arms flying through the air at her station. There, coming up the stairs! Her hands, already sweaty, gripped her controllers harder and pushed down the trigger buttons. She started firing wildly at the same moment that Alex and their teammates did.

"I'm hit!" Cat yelled as the opposing team got off a few shots at her. She focused and fired back, moving back and forth to make herself a more difficult target. She kept firing. "Got one down!"

"I've got— Ah no!" One of their randoms cursed. Cat didn't blame them. They'd gotten downed and eliminated from the match. Another of their teammates took down two opponents before going down themselves in a fiery grenade inferno alongside their third random teammate. Now it was just two on two. Cat and Alex versus two members from the final opposing team, with gear just as high-level as theirs.

This was going to be tough.

"I'm going to flank them!" Cat shouted to Alex, leaping over the walls of their once-safe bunker. Alex didn't respond—he must have been concentrating hard. Cat decided she would keep quiet so as not to disturb his jam.

Cat ran around the outer wall of the settlement, keeping her ears open for the final two combatants. This was it—she was so close to that Quest item. She just needed to keep it together for a couple more minutes—

She was being shot at! Cat saw a bullet whiz past her avatar's ear and she spun around so fast she almost got VR vertigo. Spraying bullets wildly, she somehow managed to down her opponent before she even had eyes on them—they must have already been low on health from an earlier fight.

"Yeah!" Cat yelled. "Alex, this is it; we've just got to take down one—"

Thwump. Cat's character was caught by a sniper. She was *dangerously* low on health.

"Sniper! Above!" she called out to her brother over the mic.

"I see them, I see them . . . ," Alex muttered back, much calmer than Cat felt.

"Get behind them; I'm going head-on!" Cat called out, racing up toward the highest building on the settlement, dodging shots from the sniper.

"Yep!" agreed Alex, sneaking up on their final opponent from the other direction.

"This is it!" Cat gritted her teeth as her avatar crested the final roofline. She and her enemy were face-to-face—this was the only thing standing in the way of a massive success for their Quest list. Cat opened fire and—

"I'm down! I'm down?!" she yelled in disbelief. The sniper had been amazingly accurate. Cat felt devastated. She'd been so close to victory. She could taste it. It was right there . . .

WINNER!

The bright letters flashed across Cat's screen, shocking her out of her self-pity. What?

What?

"What?!" Cat shouted.

"I got them," Alex said calmly. "I did it. I got them."

"What?!" Cat repeated, sure she must be

somehow simultaneously seeing and hearing incorrectly. "What?!"

"We won." Alex sounded happy for the first time since the match began. "We won!"

Cat yanked off her headset. They won.

They won!

So . . . why did Cat feel . . . kind of bad? She'd been preparing for this moment for weeks. This was exactly what she wanted. She had a stranger tape their team's victory dance—their randoms, it turned out, were three ladies who looked like they were probably Cat's mom's age. They exchanged social media information so they could all get Quest credit for the video, and Alex uploaded it to the app (while also getting reassurance from Cat that she still had their Hall M passes). It all happened so fast Cat could barely process it before they were shuffled out of the play area and back into the masses on the con floor.

They won.

Cat should be happy, right?

So . . . why was she definitely about to snap at her brother for no reason?

"I need to sit down," Cat said abruptly, making her way to the nearest wall. She put her back against it and slid down to the floor, her head between her knees.

"Are you okay? Do you feel sick? That's how I usually feel after VR," Alex said sympathetically, sitting down next to his sister. He patted her knee awkwardly. Alex was never great with physical reassurances.

"I'm fine," Cat said, sounding definitely not fine. "I'm fine!" Nope, not that time, either. She sighed. "I'm glad you won the game. Really."

Alex frowned. "*We* won the game."

"Right," Cat said, forcing a smile onto her face. She shoved her growing feeling of disappointment and frustration down, reminding herself where she was. This was *GeekiCon*, and they'd just gotten another forty entire points for the Quest. She was totally and absolutely for sure fine. Definitely not upset with Alex at all for any reason. For sure not feeling the way she did whenever she so much as thought about Team Dangermaker. "*We* won. Go us!"

Alex was still frowning at her.

"No sitting on the con floor!" a harsh voice snapped, and both Cat and Alex snapped their heads up.

"Oh no," Cat groaned. James M., the angry staffer from the *Igor* panel, was speedwalking directly toward them. Cat started to move to her feet but wasn't fast enough—maybe the VR *had* messed with her balance a little bit. The light above them was blocked out by James M., the convention fluorescents bouncing off the top of his very shiny forehead.

"Hi again." Cat plastered on her most charming smile. "I like your fanny pack."

James M. would not be fooled by her false compliments. "*You* two." He put his hands on his hips, where Cat saw a convention walkie-talkie hanging from his belt. Not good.

"Who two?" Alex asked innocently.

"Don't move. I'm calling this in to security. Participants in the Quest will be banned from the convention grounds for life." James M. reached for his radio.

Excuse me?! "Says who?!" Cat demanded, lurching to her feet. She had to hold on to the wall behind her to keep her balance. She came up to about James M.'s mid-chest—she definitely couldn't take him in a fight. Cat knew the Quest wasn't exactly endorsed by GeekiCon, but she'd never heard of anyone being *banned* for participating. Especially not for*ever*!

"Says me, as of right now." James M. unclipped his radio and pointed it in Cat's face. "I'm *sick* of all you . . . you *Questers* and *Vigilante League* fangirls and fake geeks who've never so much as picked up a comic book in their *life*." As James M. continued, his face got redder and redder. Spit gathered in the corners of his mouth, right on top of his tiny beard. "GeekiCon used to be about *real* fans who loved *comics*. Nerds never used to be *cool*. Kids like you are *ruining* this convention, and—"

"Welp, would you look at the time? Gotta go, *byeeeee!*" Cat talked over James M. so fast and so loud that he didn't notice until too late that Cat had grabbed her brother's hand and was diving under the older man's outstretched arm.

Cat scanned the con quickly and came up with a plan. "Floating sheep! See you there in ten! Split! *Split!*" Cat dropped her brother's hand and bolted to the right. She'd meet up with her brother at the giant floating sheep balloon, advertising some new animated series, toward the end of the hall in ten minutes. James M. had no hope of catching them now—not when they were so fast and definitely not when there were two of them running in different directions!

Cat looked behind her just once as she escaped (dangerous, considering the speed at which she was moving meant she had to dodge a human every half second). Alex was already nowhere to be seen. *Perfect.* James M. was talking furiously into his walkie-talkie, looking around in frustration.

Cat's eyes met James M.'s for just one moment before she disappeared into the crowd around her. She winked. *Hexforce Legends* champion, indeed.

14. Collect the contact information of three new friends. (18 points)

15. Beat someone at *Hexforce Legends* on the convention floor. Create and capture your own victory dance. (22 points)

8

Alex bent over with his hands on his knees, desperately trying to catch his breath. A giant inflatable sheep hung over his head ominously. This was why Fi was the athlete and not Alex. He just didn't have it in him. Who would ever want to run for *fun*, anyway? To Alex, it seemed completely counterintuitive.

"You made it!" Alex looked up, still wheezing, to see Cat appear in front of him, deposited there by the crowd perpetually in motion around them. Cat's hair was even frizzier than usual now, and she'd managed to tear her cape. A few of the comics on her shoes had started to peel away. Still, Alex was happy to see her—especially since the incident with James M. had apparently made Cat forget that she was angry at him for winning that *Hexforce Legends* match. Playing had made Alex almost throw up in his headset. But he was still proud of himself for it, even if Cat had been a bit angry. Plus, they got their Quest points. They might beat Team Dangermaker. That's what it was all about in the end.

Right?

"I made it," Alex responded, standing upright. "Barely."

"Yeah, that was a close one," Cat agreed, pulling out her phone. "What was that guy even talking about, anyway?" She started to mimic the way James M. talked, all grumpy and sputtering. "I'm a *real* fan and you're all *fake* fans and *Vigilante League* sucks unless you've read *all the comics from the start* and *only I get to say who's a real fan*, and—"

"He absolutely is the worst." Alex cut his sister off. She could keep going like that all day, he knew. "But he can also kick us out of here. *Forever.*" Alex felt his hands fidgeting the way they did sometimes when he got particularly anxious. "We should be more careful."

Cat rolled her eyes but couldn't say that he was wrong. "Yeah, yeah. I guess you're right. We can be more careful." She held up her phone to

Alex. "In the meantime, I think I've found our next Quest item."

Now *that* was something Alex could concentrate on that didn't make him as nervous as lifelong expulsion from nerd heaven. "Really?"

"Really." Cat grinned. "Look behind you."

Alex turned around, one hand on his messenger bag. There, in the middle of their aisle, were three *Vigilante League* cosplayers, kindly taking photos with any fans who asked. "Number nine!"

"'Convince three *Vigilante League* cosplayers to sing "Eye of the Tiger" with you,'" Cat quoted from the app on her phone. "Thirty-seven points!"

"But how—?" Alex began to wonder aloud, before his sister pushed past him.

"Just back me up."

Alex shook his head. Cat could be so *confident*. Even though Alex was grateful she was around to handle otherwise awkward social situations like this one, it didn't make Cat any less annoying in the way she went about it. Sure, the less Alex had to talk to strangers, the better. But he thought there had to be a way for Cat to go about these things without being so . . . what was the word he got right on that spelling test last week? . . . *domineering*. Two *e*'s, one *n*. Nailed it.

Alex trailed Cat as she dove and dodged to the front of the crowd of people taking photos of the cosplayers. There was a Dark Spider, a retro Miss Paradigm, and a Captain Patriot (the version with a beard). As they were striking a very impressive power pose, Cat stopped at the edge of the crowd. She was collecting herself. *Ah*, Alex thought with an internal sigh. *We're going for strategic adorableness today.*

Cat stepped forward, her hands behind her back and her head down a little. She looked up at the cosplayers through her eyelashes. Even though he was still a bit irritated, Alex found himself holding in a laugh as he unlocked his phone. Cat had never been shy for a day in her life, but she put on the act pretty well.

"Um, hi, excuse me?" Cat's voice was barely audible over the crowd. "Can we—can I get a picture with you? Please?"

Captain Patriot broke his power pose to look over at Cat and smiled. "Why, of course, dear citizen! Anything for the sweet children of this great nation!"

"Oh, gosh, thank you so . . . so much," Cat said, her head still down. Alex felt like he was somewhere between a wave of horrible second-hand embarrassment *for* his sister and a massive laugh attack *about* his sister. This *was* a good plan. Alex was big enough to admit that. He just wished his sister would ask his opinion about these things every once in a while before launching herself headlong into them.

Still, this was happening, so Alex shouldered his way to Cat's old spot at the front of the crowd and held up his phone. This was his cue.

Cat got into place between Dark Spider and Miss Paradigm as Alex hit PLAY on his music app. The first notes of an epic guitar riff piped out of his phone's speaker. Alex cranked the volume up. He'd never heard of "Eye of the Tiger" before it came up on the Quest list, but he was a little bit obsessed with it now. He'd listened to it more than one hundred times. It was really good pump-up music for doing his math homework. He'd just hit that REPEAT button and the song would play over and over again until he didn't even really hear it anymore. He had gotten particularly excited when he and Cat and their parents were watching a movie together and the familiar melody blasted through a superhero training montage. (Alex's parents had been shocked to discover he knew every word.)

And apparently, so did everyone else, at least in this crowd. The song did exactly what the twins had expected it to—the second the crowd recognized the bop, they all started to dance along. Cat started to dance with them. It wasn't long before the *Vigilante League* cosplayers were jamming to it, too. Alex opened his camera app and hit RECORD just in time for Cat to start singing the chorus—and nobody can*not* sing the chorus to "Eye of the Tiger." It just kind of happens.

Alex watched the dance party through his phone's camera, mouthing the lyrics as they played. This was thirty-seven points! This was huge! This was Dangermaker huge!

But—wait. Something wasn't right. Were they . . . getting the lyrics wrong? Alex listened. The *Vigilante League* didn't know the lyrics to the song very well. They were getting them wrong!

Alex's hand started to shake. He grabbed his wrist with his other hand so as not to ruin the video. It was the itch. The wrong feeling. It was flooding his entire body. How could they be getting it wrong? It wasn't hard. The song wasn't difficult. And the Quest item said to sing the song. Not to sing something that kind of sounded like the song a little bit but was actually something else entirely. Why weren't they getting it right?

Alex waved one hand to get Cat's attention.

They're not singing it right, Alex mouthed, keeping quiet so as not to interrupt the video.

Cat frowned but kept dancing. *What?!* she mouthed back.

"They're not—" Alex stopped the recording and threw his phone back into his bag. "Forget it. We got it."

Cat stood there for a second as the music shut off. The watching crowd let out a disappointed *"Awww"* and started to disperse around them. Alex watched Cat thank the cosplayers in a hurry before rushing back over to him. She was never going to understand this. Alex could feel himself spiraling.

"What is *going on* with you?!" Cat demanded.

See, thought Alex. *I knew she wouldn't get it.*

"There's nothing going on with me."

"You turned the music off while we were getting the clip!" Cat swung her hands in the direction of the cosplayers, getting them caught in her cape. "If you'd kept it going, we could have even probably gotten bonus marks for style! Why'd you do that?!"

Alex just stared at his sister. Did she not *know* they had gotten it wrong? He figured if he explained it to her slowly, maybe he could make her understand.

"They weren't singing it right," he said, shaking his head. "They were ruining it."

"It doesn't matter what they were singing!" Cat shot back.

It didn't matter? It didn't *matter*? Of *course* it mattered! "Yes, it does!" Alex exploded. "Yes, it does! We'll never get full marks if they got it wrong, and if you hadn't just barged in there without asking me first—"

"Asking you first?" Cat repeated in disbelief. "Why would I ask you first?"

"You *never* ask me first," Alex responded.

"Exactly! So why would I now? We got the points! It's fine!"

"It's not *fine*, Cat, I wish you would stop *saying* that—" Alex stopped suddenly. Something was prickling at the back of his neck. He didn't get distracted often, so when he did, it usually meant there was something really wrong. He spun around.

A few of the people from the crowd who'd been videoing the "Eye of the Tiger" dance party were now videoing *them*. Alex froze in place.

Cat peered around her brother's head. "Excuse me? A little privacy here?"

The gawkers stood there for a second, unsure

of how to react to this very loud, extremely brash, costumed twelve-year-old.

"I said *beat it*, you creeps! I know a con staff member! You want me to call James M. on the phone *right now* because I *will*—"

That was enough to get the small crowd to disperse. Alex had a sinking feeling in his stomach. He fished his cell phone back out of his bag and opened social media.

And sure enough, right there under the #VigilanteLeague hashtag: "kids in *Vigilante League* video have GeekiCon meltdown!" And reposted on another account: "This is why you shouldn't bring your kids to GeekiCon." And again: "Nerd throws a tantrum over *Vigilante League* stunt." Great.

Just great.

At least Cat had stopped the privacy snatchers before they'd gotten anything else. And the distraction had served to snap Alex out of his sneaky itch spiral. That was good. Probably.

Alex reported the video (they were kids being filmed without permission—definitely against the rules) before locking his phone and tucking it into his pocket, determined to forget about the trolls online. It wouldn't last; the video had to get taken down. He reached out and grabbed one of Cat's hands, pulling her to the side of the aisle.

"Hey. Thank you for stopping that," Alex said, looking his sister in the eye.

"No problem." Cat shook his appreciation off like what she'd done really was nothing, when Alex knew he could never have done as much. "Listen," Cat added hesitantly. "Maybe I should have asked you before jumping into that. Maybe we could have prepared them with lyric sheets or something. I didn't even think about it and I'm sorry."

Alex looked down at the floor. "Thanks, Cat. I'm sorry I . . . lost control."

"Hey," Cat said strongly, shaking her brother through their still-clasped hands. "No. Don't say stuff like that. The Quest is stressful and Geeki-Con is a lot. We're having an adventure. I still have our Hall M passes. And we're definitely and absolutely totally going to get through this. Okay?"

"Yeah." Alex looked up and smiled. He felt more determined than ever to prove to the entire world that they could do this. "And we're going to win."

9. Convince three *Vigilante League* cosplayers to sing "Eye of the Tiger" with you.
(37 points)

9

"Nerd throws a tantrum over *Vigilante League* stunt!" *Okay, first of all,* Fi thought as she tried her best to rush through the crush of smelly, sweaty bodies, *only I get to call my brother a nerd.* Though Fi was pretty riled up over the blatant invasion of privacy her younger siblings had just been involved in, one sort of good thing had come of it: As Fi had scrolled past the video of the twins singing their favorite TV show theme song in front of a large crowd (*Ducky McFowl*, obviously) and had found the "meltdown" video (moments before it was wiped from the internet after a storm of enraged parents demanded it), she'd noticed something. Right over the twins' heads in the video of their argument (of *course* they would even manage to embarrass her online) was a giant inflatable sheep. Fi had seen that sheep hanging in the air over the convention floor, and she was zooming back toward it as fast as she could.

Well, like, way slower than she could, frankly. Yes, she'd made varsity soccer, and she was only in the ninth grade. But she could only go as fast as this con would let her.

For every slow walker she swerved around and every impromptu photo shoot she narrowly avoided ruining, Fi reminded herself of why she was doing this. Dodge an elbow—*Ethan might notice me.* Avoid collision with a gigantic backpack—*on the for-sure chaperoned camping trip.* Shove through another long line—*which Mom and Dad will let me go on.*

And suddenly, like a beacon of hope, there was the inflatable sheep, in the not-too-distant distance. It was just a few more aisles ahead. Fi kept her eyes on the sheep as she surged forward. The twins were there and so was her future. Just two more aisles to go. Just one—

Wham. Fi had made the worst mistake you can make at GeekiCon—she'd stopped watching the crowd directly in front of her and had slammed into another attendee. Fi'd been moving so fast that the collision landed her straight on her butt.

"Watch where you're *going*—" said the stranger.

"Oh, I'm so sorry—" started Fi.

Both Fi and the person she'd smacked into started talking at the same time. Fi stopped mid-accusation while rubbing her head when she saw a hand with rainbow-painted nails outstretched in front of her. Fi followed the line of the hand up its arm, past the bright-blue printed shirt, to land on the face of its owner. A face with heavy eyeliner and bright-orange lips topped off with a shock of purple hair. A face Fi recognized.

Rowan Reyes. Fi was shocked to see she'd actually run into someone she actually *knew*.

Mortifying.

Completely horrifying.

If Rowan told anyone at their school that she'd seen Fi here this weekend—

But then, Fi remembered, nobody going on the totally chaperoned camping trip even *knew* Rowan. She was their class loner, always wearing stuff like boys' suits from thrift shops and dyeing her hair random colors, usually skateboarding around with giant headphones on instead of talking to people. Though the hair color thing was pretty cute and the purple did suit her. Her parents were Filipino, and Fi heard she even spoke fluent Tagalog. Rowan had just started school this past year—Fi'd heard a rumor that Rowan had been in a *cult* before this.

And she certainly looked the part now. Rowan was wearing a denim vest over her blue button-down and a fanny pack shaped like a stuffed bear—both of which, Fi realized in abject sadness, she recognized from *Star Worlds*. I mean, sure, Rowan looked better in the vest than, like, 90 percent of the other costumed dorks here. But still. Would Fi *never* be free of this weirdness?

Well, she wasn't going to be rude for no reason. Fi grabbed the offered hand, and Rowan helped haul Fi to her feet.

"Oh, dude," Rowan said surprised. "Fiorella, right? From third period."

"Fi," she answered quickly. Nobody called her by her full name except teachers. "Yeah, third period. Rowan?"

"Yeah." The girl smiled, yanking off her ever-present headphones and resting them around her neck. "So rad to see you here. This is the best place on Earth, isn't it? All your people in one place. I didn't think you were into this stuff."

Oh no, thought Fi in a panic. "Oh, I'm *definitely* not," she said, wanting to correct Rowan before the wrong word started to get around. "I'm babysitting my sister and brother. I'd never be into something like *Star Worlds;* I actually have friends."

Fi realized she'd probably been unnecessarily harsh in her rush to retain the appearance of coolness. She tried *so hard* to be different from the rest of her family, to be *cool*. But Fi saw Rowan's expression change in an instant, regardless.

"Right," Rowan said dryly, dropping Fi's hand like it was on fire. "At least I'm not cosplaying a Real Housewife of San Diego."

Fi looked down at her mother's coffee-stained leopard shirt. Suddenly she wasn't so sorry for being harsh. "This is my *mom's* shirt, actually, and even if she *does* have terrible Slovakian style, she's still kind of nerd famous!" Take *that*, nerd.

"Riiiight," Rowan said, the sarcasm dripping off every extended syllable. Rowan started to look around Fi, searching for an easy way to join the crowd around her and move on.

"I swear," Fi shot back, indignant. "You can Google her. She and my dad invented *Ducky McFowl*."

Now *that* got Rowan's attention. Her eyes

snapped back to focus on Fi through her purple bangs. "No way." Rowan got out her phone, and Fi could see her immediately opening her internet browser.

Fi smirked. "Yes way. So—" Suddenly, behind Rowan's bent head, Fi saw the inflatable sheep hanging in the air again. They were almost directly beneath it. But . . . "Shoot. Shoot, *shoot!*"

"Dude." Rowan was still deep in her phone. "Your mom's *Anna Gallo*? She's, like, a cult *hero*; I *love* that show; what the *heck*—?"

"I gotta go," Fi said in a rush. There were no twins here. No twins to be found. No twins of any kind anywhere in any sort of proximity to here. Fi was still totally screwed. And she'd gotten so distracted and forgotten . . .

"Wait, where?" Rowan asked, tucking her phone into her vest pocket.

Fi groaned. She didn't have time for this. "I told you, I'm babysitting two monstrous nerds, and I can't find them anywhere, and my parents are going to *kill* me, and if I'm *dead* they're *never* going to let me go to Kumeyaay Lake—"

Rowan snorted. It was totally gross and not even a little bit cute. "You're going to that? I heard it isn't even going to be chaperoned—"

"*Yes, it is!*" Fi snapped back while unlocking

her phone. Back to desperately combing social media.

"You need to chill—"

Fi kept frantically scrolling through her feed and groaned. "Why are they on this ridiculous *quest*—?"

"Quest?" Rowan repeated. "Look here." Rowan grabbed Fi's chin between two of her fingers and lifted her face away from her phone. Fi's heart beat a little faster, and her neck felt hot where Rowan's thumb rested. Fi jerked her chin out from between Rowan's fingers. She barely even knew this girl. Why was she acting like they were anywhere near friendly enough to touch like that? "I'll help you find your sister and brother, and in return you can introduce me to your super-cool mom. Okay? I wanna work in animation one day."

Fi paused for a second. She stared into Rowan's dorky but totally earnest face. The sooner she found the twins, Fi reasoned, the sooner she could leave this place and get back to planning her trip. And Rowan *did* seem to know her way around the con . . .

"Okay." Fi nodded as Rowan's hand dropped away. "You help me, I'll help you, and this day can end. And I can get back to Ethan."

"You got it, Leoparda," Rowan cracked. "Who's Ethan?"

"Who's Leoparda?" Cat countered.

"She was on this cartoon in the eighties—" Rowan stopped herself. "It doesn't matter. Give me your phone; let's get looking."

21. How many people can you get to sing your favorite TV show theme song at once?
(39 points)

10

If there was such a thing as a torture chamber in the middle of GeekiCon, this would have been it. Cat and her brother were hanging out at the LEGO pit. Alex knelt next to it, but Cat was knee-deep in the tiny little bricks, laying low for the time being. Her brother was happier than she'd probably ever seen him in their entire lives—she could have disappeared and he wouldn't have noticed for hours, for sure. Alex loooooved LEGOs. But every time Cat took a step in the LEGO pit, at *least* three of the little bricks got wedged into her hand-decorated shoes, and under her feet, and oh my *gosh*, it hurt *so much*.

"Cat!" Alex yelled over the din of the crowd and of clinking LEGOs. "Check it out!"

Cat looked over. They'd been hiding out in the pit, trying to avoid attention from James M. and from Fi and from their parents and from Team Dangermaker and from online trolls . . . There was a *lot* going on. Still, Cat smiled when she saw that Alex had come across someone making a life-sized replica of the *Wormhole* device.

"Now—*ow!*—that's pretty—*ouch, shoot*—cool!" Cat said, her words punctuated by LEGO pain as she shuffled gingerly over to her brother.

"I know," said Alex, still staring at the guy's sculpture in progress. "Look at the way his pattern with the orange bricks is so detailed and realistic—"

Cat wasn't really listening—she yanked her phone out of her purse and was opening the Quest app again to scroll through their remaining items.

"We still have a lot left," she interrupted Alex mid-thought. "We gotta get going."

"In a minute." Alex waved Cat off, still focused on the LEGOs.

"Or now?" Cat urged him. Didn't he realize they had a ton more Quest items to get through? Cat was getting more and more hyped up the longer she looked at the list. They had a long way to go before the end of the day, and some of these items were hard. Like *ridiculously*, *epically* hard. The longer they waited, the worse things were going to get! Cat could feel their potential future win slipping through her fingers—right into Team Dangermaker's lap!

"It was your idea to come here," Alex reminded her, still distracted.

"Yeah—and now it's my idea to leave here and do *more Questing*—"

"Are you hungry?" Alex mused, peering closer at the LEGO creation.

"Hungry?!" Cat repeated incredulously. The LEGO pit had served its purpose—it was time to move on! Immediately! Instantaneously! Big things awaited and et cetera and such! "How can you think of food at a time like this? You didn't stand up for us at all during the filming fiasco, and I'm feeling like the only person who actually *cares* about the Quest right now and—" Cat threw her hands in the air dramatically. "Actually, you know what, Alex? I *am* hungry! I'm hungry for a *win*! So let's *go*—"

That got Alex to turn around. *Finally.* "You don't have to get all Miss Paradigm on me."

"Excuse me—"

Alex sighed and moved to help Cat out of the LEGO pit. Cat could tell he was bummed about it. "Fine, fine. Let's go. Sorry I stopped to enjoy something for five minutes."

Cat clambered out of the pit. Finally. Freedom! "This is *GeekiCon*, Alex," she said, taking off one of her shoes. "This is the *Quest*." Hopping up and down on one foot, she shook several LEGOs loose from her decoupaged loafer. "The *Quest*! The most important thing we've ever done! The key to, like, our whole future! It's not supposed to be *fun*, it's supposed to be—"

Cat stopped herself, one leg in the air, balanced precariously on the edge of the LEGO pit. Alex had crossed his arms and was giving her one of those looks. You know, those classic Alex looks that only Alex could give that made her feel like a total space case for, like, *no* reason except usually because she was being a total space case.

Cat thought for two seconds about what she'd just been saying and realized why Alex was giving her the Look. She dropped her shoe onto the ground, and Alex lifted out an arm for support, raising one of his eyebrows at the same time. The final stage of the Look.

You win this round, Alex. You win this round.

"Okay," Cat admitted, grabbing hold of her

brother's arm to wiggle her shoe back on. The decoupage certainly didn't make them fit any more comfortably, that was for sure. "You're right."

"I didn't say anything," Alex said, with *way* too much innocence.

"Shut up." Cat rolled her eyes good-naturedly.

"I just *said* I didn't say anything—"

"You know what I mean," she said, dropping his arm before giving it a little punch. Alex rubbed it even though she'd barely touched him. *Now* who was being dramatic?

"Do you still have the Hall M—?"

"*Yes*. Okay, look." Cat made a big show of putting her phone into her bag and doing up the zipper. "No more phone. No more Quest. But *just* for the next half hour." Cat caught her stomach grumbling and covered her mouth with one of her hands. "I guess we *do* need to eat, anyway."

Alex gave his sister a grateful smile. "Cool. It's been a long day. And . . ." He drew the sentence out to create maximum tension.

". . . Aaaaand?" Cat repeated, trying to drag it out of him. She hated when he made her guess things, which happened pretty much every single day all the time.

Pausing just one more moment for effect (seriously, dramatic maximum!), Alex whipped open the top of his messenger bag. "I had Mom pack us *sandwiches*."

Cat laughed. Only Alex would get *that* stoked on sandwiches. "Nice one."

The twins looked both ways before crossing the busy aisle in front of them and headed up an escalator. They found a little outdoor area by one of the food vendors and settled down on the closest bit of vacant concrete they could find. Cat settled her cape around her like a blanket as Alex pulled out his fabled sandwiches.

"Peanut butter and cucumber?" Cat made a face. So nasty.

"Only for me," Alex said, clutching that one close to his chest. "I'd never let you eat my amazing lunch, anyway. You get boring ham."

"Sweet, safe ham," Cat sang, snatching the sandwich from his hand. "Hey, pass me one of those mustards, nerd," she demanded, sticking out her hand.

Alex slapped a tiny condiment packet into it, one of a bunch they'd scooped up at the vendor along with some napkins. (Cat had a costume to protect here!) Cat squirted mustard onto her ham sandwich and smooshed it back together. She wiggled her butt on the floor and closed her eyes when she bit down. She really *was* hungry. They'd been running around all day, and she hadn't even realized it!

Cat and her brother sat in comfortable silence while they ate. It was one of Cat's favorite things about time with Alex. They talked a lot—okay, *she* talked a lot, mostly—and they were *always* chatting (and sometimes arguing) about whichever new book or comic or TV show or movie they were super into at the moment. Don't even get Cat started on her ships and OTPs. There were too many to name. But Cat also really dug that she and Alex could just sit together and eat sandwiches or watch shows without it being weird or awkward. Sometimes if you tried to just have quiet time around other people they *totally* made it weird and awkward. But not Alex. The two of them knew each other so well they could just sort of hang out and *be*. Even if he did drive Cat up the wall sometimes.

Cat took the opportunity to do some people-watching as she munched away on her delicious and mustardy sandwich. (Seriously, who even invented mustard? Genius level, Cat decided.) There was literally no other place in the world like GeekiCon. Sure, other conventions were cool and the people were really nice, but there was something about *this* con that really made people bring their A game. Maybe it was that it was the biggest convention in the world, or maybe it was that they just knew this is where everyone *else* would be doing the most and it made everyone want to step it up. Like some epic feedback loop of nerdiness. Either way, Cat was astounded by every single cosplayer who walked by her. She stared at Dark Spiders, snapped a sandwich selfie, complimented an entire group dressed up as the Heroes of Justice, and even asked to take a picture of a passing imitation Normageddon. Seeing all the hard work and talent that went into these costumes made Cat want to step up her costuming game, too. Maybe this was the year she asked her parents to get her a heat gun for molding Worbla. They would totally go for that, right?

Totally.

"Ta-da!" Alex said suddenly, surprising Cat out of her GeekiCon dreamland. He was staring at Cat expectantly.

"Huh?" she responded elegantly. She grabbed a napkin and wiped at her mustardy hands before they could stain her cape.

"Get out your camera," Alex said excitedly. "Time's up!"

Time! Cat whipped her phone out of her purse and checked the clock. Sure enough, exactly a half hour had passed. She looked up and past her brother, trying to see what he was so proud of that it merited a photo.

"Oh my Igor. Alex!" Cat yelled. "Shut *up!*" Quiet time was *over*. In the space of the last half hour, while Cat had zoned out to the ham and cosplayers, Alex had been hard at work. There on the concrete beside him was a full ketchup, mustard, mayo, and relish portrait of . . .

"Wait, who is that?" Cat couldn't place the face, even though Alex was plenty talented at art (even with condiments).

Alex jerked his head to the left. "Whoever that is."

Cat looked over in the direction of Alex's gesture. Just inside the glass doors across from them was a big signing hall. At the smallest table closest to them, a guy sat alone at a table with a couple of books propped up. A little AUTHOR SIGNING NOW! board was propped up next to him. There was no line and he looked very, very bored.

But there was no doubt that Alex's portrait was bang on. And if the guy had a table, he definitely counted toward Quest item twenty-seven: "Create a portrait of your favorite convention guest out of the medium of your choice, and give it to them. Traditional art materials disallowed." Forty points!

Cat gave Alex a questioning look, and he gave her a small nod back. She threw her arms around his neck and gave him a huge hug, careful not to bump either of them into the condiment master-piece before she'd managed to photograph it.

"See?" Alex said. Cat could hear a little bit of smugness in his voice, even if she couldn't see his face. "You're not the only one who's thinking about the Quest."

Cat felt her face going red. She rocked back onto her heels—and winced. Pulling off a shoe and shaking out yet another LEGO (would it ever end?!), Cat laughed. "I guess I deserved that."

"The LEGO or my correctness?"

"Both?" offered Cat.

"Definitely both," Alex confirmed. "Come on, grab a photo and let's go give it to this guy."

"Technically, though," Cat mused aloud as she snapped a pic of her brother's mustard mas-terpiece (what *can't* mustard do, honestly), "this random guy is *not* your favorite convention guest. We for sure do not even know his name."

"I'm trying not to get so caught up on tech-nicalities," Alex said proudly. "Plus, I think he might be my favorite now. No line but still stick-ing it out with his books? That's pretty cool. I think it might just be kind of inspiring."

Cat tossed her phone at her brother. "So what you're saying is you're not getting caught up on technicalities but you've still managed to justify it so that you think it should count for full points, anyway?"

"Yes!" Alex agreed enthusiastically. Cat laughed, and they pushed through the glass doors in front of them to hopefully make Alex's new favorite convention guest smile. His ketchup creation watched them go.

27. Create a portrait of your favorite convention guest out of the medium of your choice, and give it to them. Traditional art materials disallowed. (40 points)

11

Alex felt better than he had all day. Sure, he'd had a bit of a moment with the *Vigilante League*. But he'd seen some really pro-level LEGO skills and had made that author's day with his mayo masterpiece, and *oh!* Alex even bought the guy's book. Did it sound terrible? Yes. Was Alex unlikely to read it? Okay, also yes. But he felt good for supporting an artist. That's what you did at GeekiCon. Alex hoped that one day someone at a convention would buy *his* comics out of a sense of pity and/or excitement, too. As long as people were buying them, right?

Cat seemed to be in a good place too, Alex

thought, looking over at his sister. She was buried in her phone again, submitting their Quest photos for the relish relief and the "actually eat healthy at the con" item (cucumber peanut-butter sandwiches counted as healthy in Alex's book). And she hadn't tried to order him around in at *least* fifteen minutes. That was unusually good for Cat, when he thought about it.

Yeah. *Yeah*, thought Alex, feeling like he was glowing on the inside. They were at GeekiCon, someone liked Alex's art, his messenger bag was overly full but it was fine, they were getting through the Quest . . . Yeah. Alex was convinced at this moment that life couldn't get any better.

"Hey!" an angry voice shouted from the other side of the signing hall. "You two!"

Sigh. When would Alex learn to stop thinking thoughts like that so loudly?

"Ughhhhhhh!" groaned Cat, standing on her tiptoes to see who was shouting at them. "It's you-know-who!" Alex did not know who.

"Fi?" Alex guessed.

"No."

"Dad?" Must be Dad.

"No—"

"Team Dangermaker?" Could it be—?

"No!" Cat cut him off. "It's James M.!"

Ah. "I was just messing with you; I knew all along." Alex tried his best to lie to his sister.

"Now is *not the time!*" Cat said through gritted teeth. She was looking around frantically for a quick escape. So much for chill Cat.

Well, fine. *Keep Cat chill*, thought Alex. He could handle this. Couldn't he? Yes, there wasn't a zombie horde in the world that could stop him this time. This time, *he* would be responsible for their great escape.

Wouldn't he?

But where could they go and what could they do and quick? What was happening right now . . . ? *Think, Alex, think.* Alex tried desperately to remember the con schedule in his mind. One P.M. . . . one P.M. . . . what was going on at one P.M. . . . ?

That's it! All at once, Alex remembered something that could save them. He saw it in his mind like one of those flashing bird beacons from *Epic*, the ones they made all the plushies of. Alex owned two. And he knew where he and Cat had to go.

"Follow me," said Alex, swinging his messenger bag around and heading off. He blew through the glass doors where they'd entered the hall without even waiting to see if Cat was behind him. He felt pretty cool right then. He could admit that to himself.

"'Follow me'?" Alex heard Cat repeat under her breath. Oh yeah. She was behind him.

Admittedly, this was not how things normally went down. It was usually Cat in the lead and Alex being dragged along behind her. But he was determined to try something new here, and Alex hoped he could save them.

The bird beacon wouldn't steer him wrong. Right?

As Alex blasted through the con crowd, he held his gaze just in front of his own feet. He avoided unnecessary eye contact with the people he was quickly trying to dodge and (added bonus) ensured he didn't step on anyone or anything by accident. He wasn't sure if this was how Cat managed crowds, but it seemed to work best for him. It was just about the closest Alex could get to ignoring the people around him without actually being able to ignore the people around him.

"Alex." He heard Cat shout a warning. "He's catching up! Do you even know where you're going?!" *Oh no. Oh no . . .*

They were almost there. Alex knew it was within reach. Why did he take that guy's book? His bag was so heavy now . . . just a little farther.

Left, left, down the escalator, around the corner; dodge, duck, weave, and . . .

"Here!" Alex spun, lifting his head up long enough to find Cat. They'd made it! "Get in, get in!"

"Where—?" Cat started to ask—before she realized where they were, stopping herself. "Oh. My. Darkstar."

Alex lifted his eyebrows. "One P.M.," he recited from memory, waving his sister forward and checking over her shoulder to see if James M. had spotted them yet. "*Star Cross* cosplay meetup. Outside Hall B."

They were outside Hall B. And they were on the edge of what Alex couldn't describe any way other than as an absolute sea of humans in costume.

Normally crowds were Alex's worst enemy; this one was about to be his best friend.

The cosplayers were all milling around, waiting for someone to give them some instructions about when and where and how to pose for their big group photo shoot. It was sure to be an online sensation. Alex even spotted some really unusual costumes—obscure stuff from the short-lived animated version even. *Star Cross* might have been Alex's least favorite of all the *Star* franchises, but he'd still seen every episode of every series. As he scanned the crowd for an easy way in, he especially appreciated all the *Star Cross: Big Universe Twelve* outfits. That series was obviously the best.

Even if that wasn't saying much. Well, it was no *Star Worlds*.

"I've got it, c'mon!" Alex heard Cat say beside him. *Right*. Hiding. He'd gotten them this far; he could let her take things from here. As Cat darted into a small gap in the crowd in front of him, Alex took one more look backward.

Sure enough, just as Alex was squeezing through a gap between two Heelixes, James M. rounded the corner. Alex watched the man come to a dead halt when he saw the *Star Cross* cosplayers. He thought he heard James M. say a word that his mom would *not* be pleased with—and then Alex was in the middle of the costume sea, and James M. disappeared.

For now.

Cat and Alex crouched down near a wall, using the cosplayers as cover. Alex nudged Cat as they watched the photo shoot start.

"See?" He raised his eyebrows again.

Cat craned her neck around. "See what?"

"No." Alex shook his head with a smile. "I mean, *see*? I can save us, too."

Cat rolled her eyes but smiled back. "I *know* that."

"Well." Alex paused for a second. *Huh.* "I guess now I know that, too."

"And before you ask, *yes*, I still have the Hall M passes." Cat laughed and dropped down onto her butt, throwing her back against the wall behind her. She jolted forward onto her knees nearly as quickly as she'd thrown herself backward, rubbing at her spine. "Ow, what the—?"

"Hey!" Alex peered around his sister to see what had hurt her. His eyes got big. Huge even. "Check that out!"

Cat looked up—and up, and up. It became suddenly very apparent to Alex exactly *why* this *Star Cross* photo shoot was organized here, outside Hall B, and not anywhere else in the vast convention grounds. Right on the wall the cosplayers were using as a backdrop, the con had built a *huge* replica of one wall of the *USS Venture*, the series' most iconic starship. It was made to look like one side of the ship's engine bay, all shiny metal and blinking lights. Gears and buttons and levers were sticking out at all angles—and Cat had managed to jam one right into her back. Classic Cat.

"Whoaaaa," Alex heard his sister breathe out

next to him. "And I thought the cosplayers were good entertainment value. This is wild!"

Alex nodded furiously. It was *definitely* wild. Bananas, one might even say. The attention to detail was immaculate. There was the seventh engine light, crucial to episode seven of the third season of *Star Cross: Explorer*. Over there was the deck where Senior Officer Major Davis had fainted after meeting his soul mate on Mixtar Five. And there was—

Wait.

What was that?

Alex stood up, ignoring Cat's frantic urging for him to crouch down again, lest James M. still be around. But Alex wasn't even thinking about James M. anymore. No. Now he could only focus on the fact that something on this engine bay replica . . . was wrong.

Well, not wrong maybe. But . . . different. Added?

"Cat, take a look at this," Alex said, pushing his face closer to the replica.

"What, is it germs? Because you really shouldn't get that close to anything here—"

"I think it's *writing*," Alex realized, finally reaching out to touch the replica in front of him (despite the numerous printed warnings against doing so and the potential germs, but desperate times called for desperate measures). Alex ran his fingers across one of the levers and down the side of a console.

That was it. The pattern looked so random at first, he couldn't be certain, but there was no doubting it now. There was a message hidden in the *USS Venture* replica.

And hidden messages usually meant just one thing.

Alex unzipped his messenger bag in a hurry and fished around for his phone, currently connected to one of the three portable chargers he'd brought in case of emergency battery drainage (you really can never have too many). He swiped through his folders—games, social, finance, movies . . . There! Linguistics.

He popped open his Universal Translator app and scrolled through the list of languages it held. Someday Alex wanted to make something this cool and useful but with art. He had yet to figure out what that was or how to do that. But he figured he had time.

Alex selected the *Star Cross* category and started flipping through the available languages. Not Korgon, too elegant. Not Atalantian, too boxy. Not Ioslan . . .

"DeForean!" Alex shouted triumphantly, startling Cat.

"The writing?" Cat asked, standing up to look at Alex's phone.

"The writing," Alex agreed. "This is why I always have the Universal Translator ready to go. Here, look . . ." Alex hit the video recording option in the app and passed his phone over the writing on the *Venture* console. Come on . . . *come on . . .*

Ping! The Universal Translator app had done its job. And it had done it *really well*.

"Let me see!" Cat wiggled her fingers, demanding Alex's phone. "What does it say?"

Alex looked down at the screen for one more second to be sure he hadn't misread it.

He hadn't. This was *huge*.

Alex held up his phone for his sister to read.

"DeForean. Universal Translation: Quest Item 5: The Quest donation box is hidden behind booth 3346." Cat stopped dead and stared at the phone. "Alex."

"Yes?"

"Alex!" She started to bounce in place.

"Yes?"

"*Alex!*" Cat started jumping up and down with glee, all worries about James M. forgotten.

Her purse bounced up and down against her back, and she didn't even seem to notice. "Item five! You found it!"

Well, you know what? He really had. Alex grinned. It had been a good escape plan, after all.

29. Share a photo of your team eating healthy at the convention! Maybe the most challenging item of all! (46 points)

12

"There's just no *point* to it." Fi gestured at the wildly colorful booth she and Rowan were passing.

"There *is* a point to it, dude," Rowan shot back rapidly.

"I doubt it."

"You just have to *think* about it."

"It's just a *cartoon*," Fi argued.

"I *promise* you, it's more than just a 'cartoon.'" Rowan looked mortally wounded at the very suggestion.

"It's not even in English."

"It's *even more rad* when it's not in English."

Fi laughed at Rowan's absolute and intense

certainty on this. This had been going on for the better part of an hour. Fi and Rowan were wandering around the con in search of the twins— arguing back and forth about everything the convention had on offer. Rowan loved anime; Fi didn't understand it. Fi explained her love of soccer, showing Rowan the soccer ball she always carried in her backpack; Rowan tried to relate it to her love of sci-fi. Rowan insisted Fi just had to read this comic book; Fi wouldn't be caught dead with a picture book in her bag.

But despite (because of?) the incessant back-and-forth, Fi was forced to admit that she was not *miserable*. She wasn't having *fun*, of course. Far from it. But she *was* maybe having the best time she'd had at the con all day. Which wasn't saying much, considering. But if she *did* still have to search for the terrible two, at least she had some help. Things weren't *totally* hopeless. And more importantly, it seemed like Rowan wasn't likely to rat her out to any of her friends at school.

Well, soon-to-be friends. Totally.

Fi almost tripped when Rowan held out an arm to stop her from walking any farther. Thanks to the rapid halt on the floor, someone bumped directly into Fi's back and cursed at her. Rowan flipped the dude off in response.

"Thanks." Fi laughed as the guy huffed away, complaining about con crowds. "But why'd you stop in the first place?"

"C'mon," Rowan said conspiratorially, grabbing Fi's hand. Fi's palm was sweaty. The con does that to a person.

Rowan tugged Fi over toward a corner of the anime booth they were in—why were all these cartoon girls' skirts so short, seriously?!—and tucked them into it until they weren't likely to disturb any other floor traffic. They were really close together. So close that Fi could actually smell something . . . pleasant. For the first time. All day!

"Are you wearing perfume?" Fi asked almost compulsively.

"What?" Rowan asked, distracted by her phone. "Here, check it."

Fi took Rowan's phone when she handed it over. She didn't recognize what was on the screen—some sort of checklist. "What is this?"

"Well, we weren't having any luck finding your sibs just wandering the floor," Rowan explained, "so I found their profile on the Quest app. Team DoubleTrouble."

"The Quest app," Fi repeated. She took a deep breath, letting the idea settle in her mind. "Did you just, like, have this on your phone?"

"Who doesn't?" Rowan brushed it off. "Look, we can see every time the twins upload an item—it gets crossed off their list."

Sure enough, as Fi watched Rowan's screen, she saw one of the items on the twins' Quest list stricken in real time. Number seventeen: Sneak up on one of your fellow team members and videotape the jump scare.

After all the angst the twins had caused her, the thought of Alex having the living daylights scared out of him actually made Fi smile a little.

"Can this help us find them?" Fi asked, shuffling a little closer to Rowan to get a better look at the screen.

"Every Quest team can have four members," Rowan said, pointing to the app's top bar. "Team DoubleTrouble only has two. If you register as a member and join their team, you can start completing Quest items for them and—"

"Noooooo way." Fi cut Rowan off, stepping backward and bumping into the booth's wobbly cardboard wall. She steadied it before continuing. "I am *not* becoming a member of their weird little nerdfest for kicks."

"Not for kicks, dude!" Rowan interjected. "It's a *strategy*."

Fi immediately knew where Rowan was going with this. And Fi didn't like it. It made sense, sure. But it also meant getting herself involved in one of the twins' schemes. And that was never a safe place to be.

"If I'm completing items, we'll eventually run into them?" Fi guessed.

"Heck yeah." Rowan flipped her hair out of her eyes, and Fi smelled that nice smell again. It wasn't a *bad* plan. And Fi didn't exactly have anything better on the table right now. Plus, it might get her out of here sooner. Which was a good thing. Right?

"Fine." Fi decided it was easier just to give in than to get into another argument with Rowan. "Let's go."

Rowan went to grab her phone back, but instead of snatching the cell away, Rowan wrapped her hand around Fi's. "Hang on," she said, looking right into Fi's eyes. "Before you start running again. Do me a favor and look at the folks in this booth."

Fi stared at Rowan for a second before tearing her eyes away. She glanced around the anime booth. Light-up signs screaming nonsense like *Lunar Soldier: Pretty Navy Guardian Space!* and

Igor!!! on Skates stared back at her. The booth was filled with the same weirdos who populated the rest of the con.

"They look like everyone else here." Fi shrugged. Rowan still had her hand.

"Exactly," Rowan said, infuriating Fi. She never made any sense. And why hadn't she let go?

"I don't—"

"They're *stoked*." Rowan squeezed Fi's hand and raised her eyebrows. "They're happy to be here. *Lunar Soldier* speaks to them, for whatever reason. They're around other people who get that. They can be one hundred percent themselves here without worrying about being judged or made fun of or having to explain themselves."

Fi looked back at Rowan. She looked so *earnest*. "Okay. So?"

"Okay." Rowan stepped closer to Fi. *That smell again. Lilacs?* "So what are *you* so worried about?"

17. Sneak up on one of your fellow team members and videotape the jump scare. (14 points)

13

"Boom!" Cat made an explosion motion with her hands as she dropped a toy into the Quest donation box. She'd been carrying it around all day—a special-edition *Ducky McFowl* action figure her parents had donated specifically for this charity item on the Quest list. Way to go, Team DoubleTrouble!

The hidden instructions on the *USS Venture* had led Cat and her brother straight to the donation box, tucked away beside booth 3346. Not that booth 3346 was exactly *hidden*—it was just on the side of the con floor that nobody ever really went to. You know, the one with all the body pillow vendors and independent comic-book publishers.

It wasn't their fault; it's just there were so many million trillion amazing, exciting things going on at GeekiCon that nobody really had the energy to lug around a human-sized pillow printed with their favorite alien video game character or a heavy stack of original comics.

Kind of ironic, given the whole *comics* convention thing. But it was true.

"We did it, we did it, we did it!" Cat chanted while swinging her cape around dramatically. On this side of the floor, there was enough space in the aisles to dance around majestically if you wanted to. And she wanted to!

"Do you still have the Hall M—?"

"*Yes* I do, yes I do, yes I *do*!" Not even her brother's high-functioning anxiety was going to bring Cat down right now. Not when they were crushing this Quest between their fists! Their fists of justice! They were superheroes, and the Quest was their nemesis! Wait . . . was Team Dangermaker their nemesis? Cat figured she was going to have to work on this metaphor later. When she wasn't so excited about their great success!

"What's next?" Cat asked her brother, whisking her cape in front of her face dramatically. "What do we have left?" She switched up the pose, sweeping her cape out to the side.

"Less than we should," Alex said, his brows knitting together while he checked the app.

"What do you mean?" Cat struck a third pose, nearly taking out a passerby in the process. It was all good. She was lookin' great, feelin' great.

"I mean, someone's checking items off our Quest list that we haven't completed yet," Alex said, a note of panic in his voice. He flipped the screen around to show Cat.

She dropped out of her power pose and checked her brother's phone. Frowning, she opened the app on her own phone, just in case Alex's was glitching out for some reason. But no, he was totally right. "Convince a cosplayer dressed as a character you've never heard of that you definitely know who they are" was checked off, as was "Play a sport on the main escalators." Cat knew for a fact they hadn't done either one of these. She refreshed frantically, but the poor signal inside the convention center was preventing her app from downloading the pictures and videos that had been attached to these mysterious items. So close to the answers . . . yet so far!

But the Quest team reviewed every list item as people submitted them. No one was awarded points for items falsely completed. And Team

DoubleTrouble was receiving points. So . . . what in the *Wormhole* was going on?

"Okay, what we're not going to do right now is panic," Cat said, trying to sound way more confident than she felt. "If we're getting points, then . . . someone must be helping us. Right?"

"Like . . . a GeekiCon angel?" Her brother's voice sounded shaky, and she didn't blame him. This was definitely weird.

"Like a GeekiCon angel." Cat nodded firmly. "Let's just roll with it. Why look a drift horse in the mouth, you know?"

"Gift horse," her brother corrected her.

"Well, that just makes no sense." Cat shook her head. Her brother was so smart, but he could be kind of ridiculous sometimes. "Who gifts a horse?"

"What's a drift horse?" Alex shot back.

"I just assumed it was something Mom used to have in the old country. Whatever." Cat shrugged. "Let's focus on the items that *haven't* been checked off, and worry about our drift horse later. Sound good?"

"Okay," Alex agreed tentatively. Cat sensed that he knew they had no other choice. The day was passing by quickly—way quicker than they needed it to be. They were running out of options here! And this only increased their chances of winning, really—so what difference did it make?

Right?

Right!

From out in the corridor, beyond the doors to the con floor, Cat heard something. Synth, saxophone—the unmistakable sounds of forty-year-old pop music filtered through the walls. Cat gasped with recognition.

"Dancercize!" she shouted, seemingly out of nowhere. Luckily, Alex understood immediately.

"Item twenty-two?" he asked her quickly.

"Item twenty-two," Cat confirmed, already taking off toward the sound. "'Participate in Dancercize with a Star-Trooper squad!'"

"I know what item twenty-two is!" her brother yelled as they jetted toward the con floor exit at top speed.

"Okay!" Cat yelled back, barely listening. This could be their only chance to get this item, one of the most difficult on the list. They had to follow the sound!

Cat slammed through the double doors, ignoring the protests of the volunteer guarding them. She knew Alex was hot on her trail. They were on a roll—checking off Quest items, blessed by a

GeekiCon angel. The day was theirs. She had to take advantage of this moment!

Cat rounded a corner at high speed, blisters screaming in her too-tight loafers, and headed toward the nearest set of escalators. She cursed that decoupaged-shoes Quest item with every fiber of her being. *Ouch. Ouch. Ouch* . . .

There! As Cat entered an open atrium, she saw it. A whole squadron of Star-Troopers, their white plastic armor clacking to the upbeat sounds of retro synthpop. And at the front of the force, leading them to their Quest item victory was . . .

Team Dangermaker.

Of course. Cat should have known there was only one team that could so successfully pull off such a difficult Quest item. The best team of them all. They must have been organizing this when Cat and Alex saw them with the Star-Trooper squad this morning.

And to add insult to injury, it looked like only two members of Team Dangermaker were present for this item. They must have split up to grab as many items as they could. But it was impressive that they could pull off a stunt this big with only two people. Cat had obviously never met Team Dangermaker IRL (obviously), but she was pretty sure the brown-skinned Dancercize leader (clad, of course, in head-to-toe spandex right now) was Malik, with Dahlia, their natural hair in extremely rad pastel-colored twists, filming on their phone.

Next to Cat, Alex was looking at the whole spectacle with wide eyes. There must have been fifty Star-Troopers in full exercise-video mode. Dahlia even had a speaker system to amplify their music!

Cat buried her head in her hands. There was no way they were ever going to be able to replicate this. She had been so sure of their success just a few minutes ago—and now she was crashing back down to Earth, her superhero cape tangled around her legs as she fell into the depths of the ocean. They were absolutely burned toast. Completely.

"We're never going to win," she groaned through her fingers.

Alex peeled her hands away from her face. "You know I can't hear you when you do that."

"I said, we're never going to win!" Cat repeated dejectedly, dropping her hands.

She watched as Alex forced a very fake-looking smile onto his face. "It's going to be fine!"

He was trying to help her stay positive, and Cat appreciated that. But still.

A couple of very tall, very muscular cosplayers moved in front of Cat and blocked her view of the Star-Troopers. As she started to demand they move with a loud sigh, Cat suddenly had an idea.

It was a bad idea.

It was *definitely* a bad idea.

But it was her *only* idea. And she was going to run with it. After all, they were on a roll and they *had* to keep it going. Right?

"Hi, excuse me," Cat said, tapping one of the cosplayers on the back lightly. He was shirtless and so was his friend. They had more muscles between the two of them than Cat had ever seen in her entire life. And how were they so *shiny*?

"Hello, small hero," one of the cosplayers said. Cat could tell he was committed to staying in character, even if she wasn't entirely certain of what character that was, exactly. "Do you require something of us on this fine day?"

"Yes." Cat nodded. She rubbed at the finger she'd used to tap him. *Oil.* Go figure. "I need you to . . . *distract* those two people in spandex for a minute. Just for a minute."

"How? And why?" the cosplayer asked, hoisting his ax onto the holster strapped to his back.

"The how is entirely up to you," Cat said quickly. "And the why is entirely on us. But I will give you an autographed copy of the first season of *Ducky McFowl* if you can do this for us."

His eyes went wide. Cat knew she'd struck gold. "Autographed?"

"Yep!" Cat was getting anxious now. The Star-Troopers had been Dancercizing for a while. She was running out of time!

The cosplayers only hesitated for a second before nodding in unison. "We will do this for you, small hero. Here is a card with our social media information on it. Please send us a tele-gram of the future."

"You got it," said Cat, tucking the card into her purse. "Now get out there!"

"I don't know about this—" Alex sounded anxious. Cat already knew where Alex was going with this as she watched the two buff cosplayers head off toward Malik and Dahlia.

"I *do*," Cat said forcefully, jerking her head toward the front of the Star-Trooper squad. "You tape, I'll take over. It'll just be for a second. It's all we need!"

"But it's not our item," Alex protested, following his sister anyway. "We'll get disqualified if someone finds out we piggybacked on someone else's work!"

"No one's going to notice. Come on!" she urged, getting him into place. "We gotta be fast!"

Alex shook his head but didn't say anything else. Cat knew she had him. They were going to do this!

From the shadows near the front of the troop, Cat watched as her two new oily cosplay friends stepped in between Malik and the Star-Troopers. They said something to Malik that Cat couldn't hear. Malik signaled Dahlia to stop filming. The four of them walked over to the side of the atrium for a second, their heads together.

Whatever they were talking about, it had worked! The music was still blaring—the Star-Troopers were still dancing!

Cat bolted from her hiding spot and took up position in front of them. She waved at Alex, who already had his phone up, filming. Cat did a couple of jazzy moves—arm here! Leg there! High kick! Twirl! This was it—they were going to get the item! And—

"Hey!" Cat almost felt the angry yell before she heard it. She winced and started to make a run toward Alex. An arm grabbed Cat from behind, stopping her in her tracks. She had time to mouth *Run!* at Alex before she was spun around—and found herself face-to-face with Dahlia.

Dang.

"That was *our* item!" Dahlia said, anger

contorting their face. They shifted their pink hair out of their face with the hand that wasn't on Cat's arm. "You were trying to steal credit!"

"No—I swear—" Cat protested weakly. She knew she'd been caught.

"We literally *saw* you doing it!" Dahlia looked like they couldn't believe what was happening. "That's totally not in the spirit of the Quest, man!"

Cat shook Dahlia's hand off her arm and stepped back, hands raised. This wasn't going anywhere good. "Okay. I'm sorry. I won't post it. I promise."

"Your teammate probably already did!" Dahlia protested.

Cat swallowed. They were more than likely right; Alex was nothing if not practical.

Cat's heart was pounding. It felt like it was going to slam out of her chest. Her head was hot; she might puke at, like, any second. She'd been caught cheating. And it had been all her idea. She couldn't let Team DoubleTrouble be disqualified— Alex would never forgive her. Heck, she would never forgive herself!

An idea just as bad as the one that had gotten Cat into this situation settled around her shoulders like Alex's antianxiety gravity blanket.

She couldn't. She just *couldn't*.

But she had no other choice.

"Okay, look—here," Cat said, fishing around in her purse. Cell phone charger . . . wallet . . . gum . . . Sharpie for emergency autograph moments . . . *there*. Cat pulled two pieces of paper out of her purse and held them up to Dahlia's face. "Two passes for Hall M later today. Impossible to get. So . . . so you can complete the hundred-point item."

Dahlia just stared at Cat for a second, totally shocked. "You can't be serious."

"I'm serious," Cat said. "Don't report us, and you can have the tickets."

"But these are basically impossible to get—"

"I *know*," Cat said, dropping her arm. "That's why I'm giving them to you. Just don't report me. I'm sorry. Okay?"

Dahlia only waited for a moment before holding their hand out in front of them, palm open. "Fine. We're even, then. But don't mess with Team Dangermaker again."

"Yeah. Whatever," Cat said quietly, dropping the two tickets into Dahlia's hand. She felt like she was handing over her life. And it was all her fault.

Dahlia closed their hand around the tickets with a vise grip and Cat didn't blame them. She turned around without another word—and ran almost smack-dab into her brother's face. He was right behind her.

"Alex!" Cat said. She forced a smile onto her face, just like he had before. "We did it!"

"What did Dahlia want?" Alex said, panicky. "Did they know?"

"Nobody knew, bud," Cat said. "We did it!" A second too late, she spun in a circle and struck a pose. Alex frowned. He clearly wasn't buying it. She had to distract him before he kept asking questions. Cat knew she could fix this. She *knew* she could.

She just . . . needed a little time. That was all.

5. Find the Quest donation box and drop off a toy from the convention floor. (56 points)

18. Play a sport on the main escalators. (20 points)

22. Even baddies have to stay in shape. Participate in Dancercize with a Star-Trooper squad. (44 points)

28. Convince a cosplayer dressed as a character you've never heard of that you definitely know who they are. (24 points)

14

There was something up with Cat.

Alex wasn't great with people, but his sister was the one exception to that rule. He basically spent twenty-four hours a day with her. He had since the second they were born. Alex didn't need special psychic twin powers to know when something was up with Cat.

Although, for real, it would have been pretty excellent to have special psychic twin powers.

Regardless. There was something up.

And Alex was going to find out what.

Just . . . not yet. Usually when Cat had done something wrong she tried to make up for it in really *grandiose* ways (he'd gotten that one wrong last week on the spelling test and had worked on it a lot since then, thank you very much). This time was no exception, even though he still didn't know what, specifically, Cat felt she had done wrong. Was she just trying to make herself feel less guilty about cheating?

Because she had *definitely* cheated. Alex had recorded the quick clip of Cat Dancercizing in front of the Star-Troopers and had immediately uploaded it to the Quest app before he had a chance to even think about what they were doing. Looking back, though, there was no doubt they'd stolen that item from Team Dangermaker. Cat and Alex hadn't done any of that hard work themselves. They'd just passed off what Team Dangermaker had done as their own. Extremely, incredibly unchill. The only way Alex knew how to deal with what he'd just been a part of was to . . . not think about it at all.

Thankfully, Cat's something-upness was making that part, at least, easy on Alex. They'd bolted from the atrium as soon as Cat was finished talking to Dahlia. In a stroke of socializing genius that never would have occurred to Alex, Cat DM'd one of the women who'd been on their winning *Hexforce Legends* VR team earlier in the day. She wouldn't tell Alex why, but they were now rushing to meet their new friends by the AC Comics booth on the floor.

Usually when Cat refused to tell Alex what was going on, he worried. This time, he was just looking forward to the AC booth's plush carpets. His feet could use a break from all the concrete. It had been a long day—and it was only . . .

Alex gasped as he checked his watch while fast-walking through the con crowd. It was almost three o'clock. *Three o'clock! The* Epic *signing!* And the volunteer had told them to be back there *well* before that . . .

"Cat," Alex called out weakly, but his sister was too far ahead of him to hear. How could he have forgotten about the *Epic* signing? He'd gotten so caught up with James M. and the donation box and the cheating—*don't think about it*—and Team Dangermaker that it had completely skipped his mind. His only chance to meet Adrianna Tack . . . his only chance to complete item sixteen . . . he was blowing it!

Again!

Alex sped up a little bit in the hope of stopping his sister. Sure, they were heading to see Cat's new friends or whatever, but wasn't Adrianna Tack more important?

He tried again. "Cat." Still nothing. Cat took

the last curve toward the AC booth at a breakneck pace, and Alex started to jog to keep up with
her. Why wouldn't she stop?

"Cat!" She'd finally come to a stop next to a
massive line that was snaking around the edge
of the AC Comics booth, wrapping back on itself
a few times over.

"Sorry," Cat apologized to someone in the line,
squeezing past them despite their complaints.
"'Scuse me. Comin' through." Alex was at a total
loss. Was Cat cutting into this line to find her new
friends?

*Did Cat's newfound love for cheating know no
bounds?!*

Alex clutched the strap on his messenger bag
and followed his sister with gritted teeth, making an apologetic face at the people in line he was
cutting past in her wake. Thankfully, they didn't
have to go far—Cat found the three women from
their *Hexforce Legends* win almost at the very back
of the line, just next to the lime-shirted volunteer
with the LINE CAPPED sign.

"Made it!" Cat said triumphantly. She high-
fived one of the ladies.

"Hi! So glad!" One of the other women smiled.
She turned to Alex quickly and introduced herself as Ohsa—or Ohsarry88 online. Her friends

were Kate and Wendy. They were all super-nice. But Alex had bigger fish to fry.

"Hi, I'm Alex. Cat." He tugged on his sister's sleeve to get her attention. "Do you still have the Hall M passes? And it's almost three o'clock; we have to *go*—"

Cat just stared at him for a second. She turned back to Ohsa. "We're good from here, friends. We really appreciate the help."

"Well, you got us that win earlier, so we're even now." Ohsa laughed. Alex had absolutely no idea what was going on. And Cat was ignoring him. A cheater *and* rude.

He didn't even *know* his sister anymore.

Alex watched with total confusion as Ohsa and her friends left the line, leaving Cat and Alex on their own. Just when Alex was about to repeat his previous sentiment to his sister, she pointed around the corner of the AC Comics booth.

"Just look around the corner," she said slyly.

Alex sighed. He *hated* these games. But he knew how Cat worked.

He peeked his head around the side of the booth. And he saw . . .

. . . the Pixel Comics booth next door. And the start of the line of which they were currently bringing up the rear.

The *Epic* signing line.

Cat.

Cat!

"Cat!" Alex turned around, his mouth hanging open. "How?"

Cat's sly smirk turned into a full grin. "I texted Ohsa while we were running from James M. I knew we were going to be too busy to stand in line ourselves, and I figured they would be willing to do us a solid and save us a spot in line. And I'm glad they did," Cat said, her face changing just slightly, "because this line is *really* long."

Alex took in his surroundings with fresh eyes. Just ahead was the Pixel booth, *Epic* central, the place that not only held the key to a Quest item but also one he'd been dreaming about for months on end, mindlessly drawing *Epic*'s infamous bird beacons in his sketchbook when he should have been doing his homework (or in class, or whenever he was bored). The wall of people stretched around the Pixel booth several times *and then* snaked through the center. There must have been at least two hundred people standing with their *Epic* comics and beacon bird plushies at the ready. Without VIP access, they were relegated to taking their chances with the queue. They were in before the cap but just barely. If the line didn't move fast enough to get to everyone before the hour was out . . .

"We're toast." Alex sighed. He started breathing fast again. His mood changed so quickly it might as well have been the wind by the sea outside the convention center. It felt like the weight of the cosmos was hanging around his shoulders, flattening across his chest.

"We'll be fine," Cat reassured him. "Let's kill some time. What do you have in your bag? Show me . . ."

Alex had forgotten for a moment that he was even carrying one—remarkable, considering how heavy the thing was at this point. He knew his sister was trying to distract him from his panic attack, but he didn't care—he did what she said. Alex slung his messenger bag off his shoulder and thumped it onto the ground. Kneeling down, he dug through its contents.

"Let's see," he said, mostly to himself. "That guy's book, some apples, my console, Cards for Bad People . . ."

"No, no, and no." Cat dismissed each one in turn. "Nothing else?"

"Well," Alex offered, looking up at his sister. "There's my sketch pad, I guess."

Cat's eyes lit up. "Perfect. You should sketch!"

Alex shrugged. He didn't know if it was *perfect*—it certainly wasn't going to make the line move any faster—but he pulled the pad and a charcoal pencil out of his bag and settled himself down cross-legged on the floor. Alex stretched out his neck and fit the pencil comfortably into his hand. "What do I sketch?"

"*Anything*," insisted Cat. "This is the best time killer in the world. There's so much good people-watching here. Just look around."

Cat might have been right about this one. From Alex's vantage point, there *was* a lot to draw. Forget landscapes—this was a million times cooler. There were cosplayers; people in the coolest T-shirts Alex had ever seen; huge signs for new shows; posters for exclusive toys; and, all around, the most interested and eclectic group of fans ever assembled in one place.

Instead of drawing any of the cosplayers or stars, though, Alex looked at the lime-clad girl holding the LINE CAPPED sign next to him. Her job was really important—she told people this was the end of the line. And she probably got a lot of flak for it. Alex began sketching out a little comic with the green-shirted girl as its star, holding back masses of undead with just her sign as a shield, a flower between her teeth.

Ten minutes later and well into his drawing, the volunteer looked down at him. "Heyyyyy," she said slowly. "Is that . . . is that *me*?"

Alex froze. He loved to draw, but he didn't like showing people his work. *Especially* if he was drawing them.

"Yeah, I can stop," he muttered by way of apology. He was weirding people out. He was always doing this—at school, at the park, in the grocery store, now here. *Bleh.*

"Are you kidding?" The volunteer laughed, reaching around the couple in line behind the twins to try and snatch the pad out of Alex's hands. "This is amazing. You just drew this now?"

Alex turned splotchy and red. He really, really hated when people touched him or his stuff without asking first. "That's mine." He yanked it back quickly and brought it to his chest.

"Um, he just means he likes holding his own sketchbook . . . ," Cat said. She gently tipped the book away from his chest so she could see his drawing. "But he's a great artist, right? Can I see it, Alex?"

The girl kept smiling, which made Alex feel less anxious. "Sorry." She held her hands up in front of her. "I didn't mean to grab it. This is just, like, the coolest thing that's ever happened to me," she said, still staring at the comic. "Hey, Jackson! Get over here!" she called down the line.

Another green-shirted volunteer came bounding over, a couple of friends in tow. "You rang?" He bowed jokingly.

"Check out what this kid did in line," the girl said. There was no way out of it now. Alex had to do it. He had to show a bunch of people his art. He took a deep breath and carefully ripped the little comic out. Alex handed it to the girl, who held it up to show it to her friend. Cat snapped a picture of the volunteer with her comic portrait.

"Holy wow." The second volunteer, Jackson, laughed. "Can you do me, too?"

Cat nudged Alex's shoulder, and when he looked at his sister, he was certain she had her scheming face on. *Say yeah*, she mouthed.

Easy for her to say! thought Alex.

"Yeah, sure." Alex shrugged mildly, trying to appear calmer than he felt. Sketching in front of other people was okay. Right? At least he wouldn't have to talk.

Alex got down to it. Over the next half hour, as the line inched forward almost impossibly slowly, a crowd of volunteers formed around the siblings. Alex drew sketch after sketch of volunteers doing a variety of heroic things on the con floor. When a lead staffer showed up to ask what all the fuss was about and Alex drew her as a winged centaur, she laughed until she cried.

"That's it, kid, we're taking you up," she said, wiping her eyes.

"Taking me up where?" Alex asked, confused, clutching his sketch pad.

"We're taking you *up*," she repeated, checking in quickly on her radio. "To the front of the line. Let's go, kid. You've earned this one."

Only when Alex felt Cat's hands hovering near his back was he able to start moving forward. "Uh . . ."

"Right," Cat said loudly, taking over. "That's *so* awesome of you. Thank you," she said to the girl. Then Cat leaned in close to Alex. "*You're a total genius,*" she squealed through a massive grin.

"What's happening?" Alex asked loudly. What was he supposed to do? They were going to the front . . . for what? Were they—?

As they moved toward the front, a vision emerged. It was the author and illustrator of his most favorite comic ever. Steven J. Rhys and Adrianna Tack. Adrianna Tack! Right there. Right in front of him.

Right.

Now?!

The lead volunteer slid Alex and Cat into place in front of the writer and artist with a quick explanation, showing them a few of his sketches. Alex was sure he had never been so red in his life. He figured he had probably ascended to another plane, that's how nervous and embarrassed he was in that moment. He probably was not even on Earth anymore. He was probably . . .

"You're really talented!" Adrianna Tack herself brought Alex out of his starry-eyed stupor. "What's your name?"

Alex just stood there, stunned.

"Alex," Cat offered, from just beside him. "He's a big fan. The biggest."

"Aren't you a little young for *Epic*?" Steven J. Rhys laughed.

"It's—" Alex's voice cracked, and he cleared his throat, his face going all blotchy and red again as he attempted to actually make coherent sense. "It's the most brilliant space opera I've ever seen. It's *Romeo and Juliet*, but if they were both aliens in an intergalactic conflict. It's the most human story ever, even though none of the characters are human. It's helped me understand a lot about people and how to interact with people and feelings, and I just . . . really love it," Alex said, his words tumbling out in a rush, knowing that if he stopped he would never be able to start again. It was maybe the longest sentence he'd said out loud in ages. And Adrianna Tack was looking *right at him*.

With a smile, Steven shook his head. "You know what, who am I to turn down a fan? Let me sign one of these for you," he said, bending over an issue of *Epic*.

"Can you write 'Team DoubleTrouble' on there, too?" Alex heard Cat whisper to Steven from beside him.

"Hey, can I keep this?" asked Adrianna. She was holding one of Alex's sketches.

"You . . . want my art?" asked Alex, his shock overcoming his nerves.

"Only if you'll sign it for me!" She smiled back.

Yep, he had definitely ascended. With a shaking hand, Alex reached out and grabbed the Sharpie Adrianna offered him, scribbling his signature onto the bottom of the paper. When he gave back the Sharpie, she handed him back his *Epic*, also signed.

"Keep drawing," Adrianna said, looking Alex right in the eye. "One day, you'll be sitting in *my* seat."

And with that, the lead volunteer pulled them

away from the line and back into the crowd with some quick thank-yous and goodbyes. Alex barely looked up from his shiny new signature even for a moment, his heart so full of elation that he completely forgot where he was, just for a moment.

"You okay?" Cat asked.

Alex tore his eyes away from his signed comic to look at his sister. "Are you kidding?"

Cat pulled out her phone again, snapped a pic of the signatures, and uploaded it to the Quest app. She looked up at Alex with a triumphant grin before, suddenly, the expression on Cat's face changed to one of pure terror.

"James M., down the hall!"

It was time to run again.

But not before Alex carefully tucked the *Epic* comic back into its bag and board and put it safely away in his messenger bag. He had his priorities straight, after all.

16. Get a real-life comic-book artist to sign your team name in their own comic. (76 points)

23. High-five another Quest team. How high can you go, actually? (30 points)

15

Fi would never say she was having a good time. Not out loud. Maybe, if someone were to threaten Fi with the worst thing imaginable—like, say, never being allowed to go camping unchaperoned again—then *maybe*. But under any other circumstances, she would never, ever admit it.

But internally, totally secretly, between Fi and Fi . . . she was maybe, just maybe, having a good time completing Quest items with Rowan.

Ugh. It was gross. But it was true.

Fi had tried to convince a cosplayer she knew who they were even though she obviously had no idea (item twenty-eight, twenty-four points). Rowan got a good laugh out of that one. But Fi had gotten her cool vibe back by impressively bouncing her always-handy soccer ball knee to knee while ascending the con's big main escalator (item eighteen, twenty points). Now they were sitting on the con floor—they'd found a booth with super-plush comfy carpets for their butts—and were working on item eleven: Write a poem for someone you see on the con floor who looks like they could use a pick-me-up. Rowan, feet flat on the floor, was digging through her fanny pack for a pen. They were planning on giving their poem to a very tired-looking AC Comics volunteer.

Fi, exhausted, leaned her head onto Rowan's shoulder. She had determined the nice smell was Rowan's hair and was happy to use it to mask what Rowan called the "con funk" whenever she could. Fi sighed deeply and took a second to relax.

"You know," Rowan said with a small smile, coming up triumphantly with the pen, "you can admit you're having fun."

"I am not!" protested Fi, lifting her head up again and trying to snatch away the pen unsuccessfully. She couldn't help but laugh as she said it, though.

"You are!" Rowan jabbed Fi with her pen, and her purple bangs covered her eyes. "You are and you know it. So what's the deal?"

"There's no deal." Fi brushed her off, still smiling despite herself.

"I'm serious, dude." Rowan turned to face Fi. "Be real with me. I'll be real with you."

"I don't even know what that means. Give me that; I'll write it," Fi deflected, grabbing for the pen.

Rowan moved the pen up and away from Fi's reach. "I mean . . . okay, here. I'm going to trust you with something about me. And then maybe you can trust me with something about you. Okay?"

Fi hesitated. Rowan had been great today. Like . . . really great, actually. But did she want to go there?

Remembering that she really *did* need Rowan's help to find the twins, Fi conceded. "Okay. Go for it."

"So you know how everyone at school thinks I was in a cult."

Fi was surprised. Rowan *knew* people said that about her? Fi must have sat there with her mouth open for just a second too long, because Rowan put two fingers under Fi's chin and shut it for her.

"Yeah, I secretly kind of love that people think that about me, so I don't correct them. Reality is, natch, way less rad." Rowan laughed. "My folks are musicians. We traveled around a lot, and I was homeschooled. Now we have a real house, so I have to go to a real school."

Fi shifted, pulling her knees up and resting her head on them. "That sounds so . . . exciting."

"Sometimes," Rowan agreed. "But mostly it meant I didn't really know anybody. I didn't have any friends, you know? We never stayed anywhere long enough. Instead, I had . . ." Rowan gestured around her vaguely. "Comics and games and shows and movies. And fandom. I got totally obsessed with so many things. And then I'd go online and find other people who were *just* as obsessed with the same things. And it's, like, instant friendship. You just *get* each other. Even if you're not *around* each other, you know?"

Fi didn't know. Maybe it was like being fans of the same soccer team? Regardless, Fi liked listening to Rowan talk, so she nodded.

"The thing about that kind of friendship, fandom friendship," Rowan continued, "is that it's just completely genuine. Everybody knows exactly who you are and what you're into. You can just be yourself. No games. No garbage. It's huge. Fandom connects people all over the world. And then once a year, if we're lucky, we get to meet up IRL here. At GeekiCon. And it's . . . kind of magic."

Rowan made it sound like magic. A magic Fi had been missing out on. And . . . for what? Why *did* all this make her so uncomfortable?

"I never really thought about it that way," Fi said. "I guess I never really thought about it much at all—"

"No sitting in the booth!" A gruff voice interrupted Fi's thought. Rowan and Fi scrambled to grab their notepad and pen and stood in a hurry. "I said, no sitting in the—"

"We got it, we got it!" Rowan responded, just as rough.

The angry guy stormed over to them. He was older, like Fi's dad's age, and had a big CON STAFF badge around his neck. It identified him as JAMES M. "What do you two think you're doing here? Show me your passes," he demanded.

Rowan held out her badge, rolling her eyes. Fi followed suit. James M.'s examined Rowan's badge first, then Fi's. In an instant, he snatched it out of her hand, tugging her forward by the neck.

"Hey—"

"This is a GUEST badge. It says here you're a publicist. You don't look like a publicist to me," James M. said accusatorily.

All the blood drained from Fi's face as she remembered—she had grabbed her parents' publicist's badge this morning in the rush to get out of the room. It didn't really matter—nobody checked these things except to make sure you had a badge at all.

Except for this guy, Fi thought with growing dread.

"It's just a mistake—"

"What's your problem, anyway?" Rowan demanded, knocking Fi's badge out of James M.'s hand and stepping between them. Under her breath as she made the move, Rowan whispered, "Just go!"

Fi froze for a second. Go where?

"What's my *problem*?" James M. repeated, now visibly angry. "My *problem* is you pink-haired social justice warriors taking up space in *my* convention, disrespecting the art by sitting on the *floor* of the *AC Comics* booth when you probably couldn't even name a *single* AC Comics *character*—"

"*Now*, Fi!" Rowan hissed under her breath while James M. continued his nonsensical tirade.

Fi didn't hesitate this time. She spun on her heel and took off down one of the con aisles, James M.'s frustrated yells swallowed up by the crowd behind her. Fi never thought she'd be grateful for this giant convention crowd—but she sure was now. Rowan would find her later. She was certain of it.

She had to.

Fi had no idea where to turn, so she decided to do the only thing she could think of in the moment: keep moving forward, and as quickly as possible.

She motored around the corner of the AC Comics booth, desperately searching for something she recognized, something that could jog her memory. Fi scanned the room as best she could while continuing to avoid the crowds: super hero movie costumes, people live gaming, a girl wearing wings two times her height, a giant sign for Pixel Comics . . .

Wait.

Pixel Comics.

Fi stopped dead in her tracks, barely noticing when someone collided with her back. Why did Pixel Comics sound so familiar?

She racked her brains as hard as she could. She knew someone had mentioned it to her today. It wasn't Rowan . . .

It was Alex! That morning, while getting ready! The one thing he couldn't stop talking about!

Finally, Fi had a direction. She didn't know for sure that she would find the twins there—but it was her best bet.

Could Fi's luck finally be turning?

And was it all thanks to Rowan?

1. Write a poem for someone you see on the con floor who looks like they could use a pick-me-up. Give it to them! (24 points)

16

Not to exaggerate, but Cat was basically a hero.

Yes, she had cheated on the Quest. And *yes*, said cheating had lost her and Alex their prized Hall M passes. And *no*, Alex did not know that yet and was definitely, positively going to absolutely murder her when he found out.

But Cat had gotten Alex his *Epic* signature, and they'd completed another Quest item to boot. That was the most important thing of all to Alex, that *Epic* session, Cat reasoned. Maybe, since she was such a hero, he wouldn't be *that* angry at her for losing their Hall M passes.

Maybe.

Right?

Cat took a sidelong glance at her brother, tapping away on his console. They were seated behind a booth in Artist Alley, resting their feet while also doing a good deed (and totally coincidentally, a Quest item). After spotting James M., Cat had made a beeline straight for one of the less-populated areas of the floor. There were two big Artist Alley items on the Quest list—take a photo of your favorite artist and upload it to social media to spread the love, and then volunteer to help someone out at their booth. Cat had snapped a pic of Jess Carrell's table to upload—her art looked like a rainbow-colored Lisa Frank catalog from the 1990s had exploded all over space, and Cat was totally obsessed with it. Cat had even bought one of her pins while she was there, a small purple cat connected to a speech bubble that simply said GO AWAY. Purrfect.

For the next item, they'd found a gal sitting alone at her table who looked like she hadn't moved in hours. Cat told her they'd be happy to man her booth while she got something to drink and hit the bathroom, and the artist had been super-grateful. They'd exchanged social media deets, and the gal and her cash-stuffed belt bag had run for the nearest ladies' room. Now Cat and Alex were greeting any folks who stopped by with the promise that the artist would be back any minute.

Seated, resting, alone. Alex had his *Epic* comic. Cat's heroism was fresh in his mind.

Welp. No time like right heckin' now, Cat reasoned. Right?

Oh, Miss Paradigm. This was going to be awful.

"Sayyyyy, Alex!" Cat said, falsely bright. She turned to her brother with a huge smile on her face. "How about that *Epic* comic, huh?!"

"Are you finally going to tell me what's been up with you?" Alex said mildly, not bothering to look up from his game.

Cat swallowed. Could the whole con hear that swallow? It basically echoed in her ears. "Oh, uh, yeah, totally! Can't believe you knew something was up."

"You *know* I knew something was up," Alex said, hitting the PAUSE button on his console. He looked up. "Okay, I'm ready."

"Okay, me too," Cat lied. "So remember the thing with the Star-Troopers?"

"You cheated."

"Yes, cool, okay, you totally remember." Cat

couldn't make her leg stop bouncing up and down. Why did it always do that? "So Dahlia noticed me. Doing that. Cheating."

"I figured as much." Alex shrugged. "I've been trying really, really hard not to think about what that meant."

"I understand." Up and down. Up and down. Up and down. "Well, and it's not even a big deal." Cat tried her best to sound casual. "It's, like, it's basically nothing. It's like nothing happened, really, at all, actually."

"You want to tell me that nothing happened?" Alex was not having this.

"No." Cat shook her head. "One *tiny* thing happened. I had to—"

"I'm back!" said a cheerful voice from across the table. Oh, right. The gal. Who owned this table. And all the art on it. Was back!

"Great! Oh, great!" Cat stood up so fast she knocked her chair over. Alex just stared at her for a second before tucking away his console and standing up, too. He set Cat's chair back upright.

Cat climbed out from behind the booth and wiped her sweaty palms on her cape before shaking the gal's hand. "Thanks so much."

"No, thank you! I can't tell you how much I

needed the break. Take a pin," she offered, holding out one of her cute *Whom, M.D.* designs. Alex took it immediately, thanking her.

Cat and Alex walked out into the main aisle of Artist Alley. Cat's leg was bouncing even though she was standing up now. Her brain was just one giant scream. She couldn't keep doing this. She had to get it out. She had to—

"So what were you going to—?"

"I lost our Hall M passes!" Cat blurted out so fast she barely registered it was happening.

Cat slapped her hand over her mouth and stared at her brother in horror. It was out there. She'd had to admit it. He knew. He *knew*.

It was going to be fine. He wasn't going to be angry. Alex never got angry—

"You *what*?!"

Okay. Alex was angry. Cat registered that Alex had continued talking (*definitely angry*) but started running through options in her head. What was the best damage control in this scenario? And were things really *so bad*, anyway?!

That was it. She just had to help Alex see *logic*; that was all. Alex loved logic.

"I know!" Cat interrupted her brother, who was still on his *very angry mile-a-minute* tirade.

"Okay, I know. I messed up. I'm sorry. But look!" Cat gestured toward Alex's messenger bag. "I figured out how to get your *Epic* comic signed! You met Adrianna Tack!"

Alex swung his messenger bag away from Cat's view and looked at her like she'd just committed the worst sort of betrayal. "Are you really going to use Adrianna Tack to try to make me feel better about this?"

Yes? "No?"

"Because it's not going to work!" Aaaaand there he went again. Cat knew everything Alex was spouting had an element of truth to it—she *did* need to be more organized and responsible; it was only on, like, *every* report card she'd ever gotten—but it wasn't *helping* anything.

"I just think"—Cat cut her brother off again and tried to sound like one of the "wellness influencers" she sometimes came across online—"that what we really need to focus on right now is *positivity*."

"Is that going to positively bring back our Hall M passes?" Alex demanded.

Cat stared at him. "Maybe?"

Alex just shook his head. "I can tell you're not even listening to me."

"I am!" Cat insisted loudly. She could tell the artists in the booths near the aisle were starting to look at them weird. Usually that wouldn't bother Cat at a con, but . . . it kind of did, right now. "I am," she said again, quieter this time.

"Good. Because . . . because you know what, Cat?" She could tell Alex was struggling with whatever he was about to say next by the way his hands kept fiddling with the bag strap.

"What?"

Alex took a deep breath, his hands clutching tight around the woven strap across his chest. "Even since before the *Vigilante League* thing, you've been just telling me what to do. You haven't asked what I want to do even *once*. And actually, the Quest just isn't any *fun* anymore."

Cat couldn't believe what she was hearing. "Telling you what to do?" she repeated, shocked. "I'm not *telling you what to do*; I'm just trying to get our Quest items done! I'm fighting for both of us here, since you don't seem interested!" Cat was getting louder and louder and she couldn't stop herself—she was so angry now! "I'm doing this for *you*—so you can get that mentorship!"

"Stop it!" Alex, usually so quiet, now matched Cat's tone. "You're doing this for *you*—so you can hang out with Corwin Blake and be just as cool online as Team Dangermaker. Don't lie to me, Cat. It doesn't work."

Cat swallowed around a huge lump that had just formed in her throat and steadied her voice. "You don't know what you're talking about."

But he did. Alex always did.

6. Volunteer to help at an Artist Alley booth that is definitely not yours. (35 points)

31. Post about your new favorite artist from Artist Alley on your social media.
(31 points)

17

Alex rushed to catch up as Cat stormed ahead in a huff. Always so *dramatic*. He shook his head.

"You don't care about the Quest at all, and I'm trying to help you get this big thing. I thought you would be *grateful*!" Cat said over her shoulder as she stormed down another aisle. Alex watched her cape swish back and forth behind her, like it was punctuating her point.

Well, her point *sucked*. Take that, cape.

"I've been working just as hard at the Quest as you have!" Alex shot back. How Cat could think otherwise was totally insulting to Alex. Hadn't he won them the *Hexforce Legends* VR challenge?

And even gone along with her horrible cheating plan?

Wait.

The cheating plan.

Cat's horrible cheating!

Alex could feel the puzzle pieces sliding together in his head. It was like one of those slide puzzles he was really good at, except now he hated it. Alex stopped dead in front of a colorful booth almost ceiling high with weird drawings of anime girls. Cat didn't notice at first and kept walking. She only turned back when she saw her brother wasn't next to her anymore.

Alex watched her turn. *Please don't let this be true*, Alex thought. *Please, please, please.*

"Cat," he said slowly, "when you say you 'lost' our passes . . . did you 'lose' them . . . to Team Dangermaker?"

The words rang out into the din of the con and seemed to echo between the two siblings. There were a million noises around them—people laughing, artists chatting, videos blaring, the background roar of the con in full effect—but the only thing Alex could hear was Cat's total and absolute silence.

It was deafening.

"Um." Cat just swallowed and stood there, frozen. Alex didn't move, either.

"Answer me, Cat." He was being forceful now. That was something he could do. With Cat, at least.

". . . Yeah." She nodded, looking at the ground. That was usually Alex's deal, yet here they were. "Yeah, I did. I gave them to Dahlia. I had to."

Alex couldn't believe what he was hearing. He couldn't *believe* it. He needed a minute. He needed a minute to deal with this. Alex sat down on the floor in front of the weird anime booth, landing hard and ignoring the complaints of the people perusing the wares. They could walk around him.

"How—" he started to ask before being cut off. *As usual.*

"I had to," Cat repeated quickly, kneeling down next to him. "I had to. It was the only way to stop them from disqualifying us."

Alex covered his ears to block out the background noise. There was too much going on. This was too much. "You only *had to* because you *cheated* in the first place!"

"I know!" Cat slumped down onto the ground next to Alex and put her head in her hands. "I know. I messed up. But you have your signature—"

"Stop bringing that up! I helped with that, too; I got us to the front of the line!" Alex squeezed his ears harder. Cat was just making things *worse*.

"I'm sorry—"

Alex couldn't handle it anymore. Cat couldn't stop making things worse for herself and for them! Alex stood up abruptly and dropped his hands back to his messenger bag strap. "I can't be here right now," he said to no one in particular. Looking down at his sister, Alex added, "Don't follow me."

He'd never felt so betrayed in his entire life. Cat had messed up their entire day—their entire plan—and for what? A few extra easy points? He still couldn't believe it. What was the purpose of any of this if it was just going to tear them apart?

Alex made a beeline for the floor exit and just kept walking once he was out in the corridor. He slammed his badge against a scanner and burst through the convention center doors into the midafternoon sunlight. It was oppressively hot but Alex barely noticed. He kept walking and walking, turning a corner at the edge of the building and finally coming to a stop, resting his back against the center's concrete wall.

In front of him, he saw a horde of people making their way over to the hotel next door—Alex heard that was where the press did all their celebrity interviews. To his left, the rest of the city. And to his right—

A door.

A totally unguarded double door.

Alex stared at it for a second before turning to his messenger bag. He rooted around in it for a couple of seconds—apple, sketch pad, comic, that guy's heavier-by-the-minute book—before he found the GeekiCon guide. Flipping to the map in the center, Alex took a hard look at the convention center layout. Then he looked around. Then he looked at the map again. Back to the door. And back to the map again.

There was no doubt. Alex was certain of it. That was the press door to Hall M.

And no one was watching it.

Alex sidled over toward one of the handles and, super-casually, gave it a tug. It opened with no problem. There was a small antechamber inside, leading to a set of black curtains. Beyond that could only be Hall M. Wait until he told *Cat*—

Alex froze. He kept the door ajar in his hand.

Cat. Was he just going to forgive her for what she did? *Could* he? Or did he want to hurt Cat just as badly as she hurt him? Plus, if Alex let her in through this door right now, she might feel like what she did was right. Or like it didn't matter.

But it *did* matter. It mattered to Alex a *lot*.

A lot more than the Quest mattered to him right now.

Alex dropped the handle, and the door shut silently in front of him. He needed more time to think.

18

Fi had been running.

She was a soccer player, so no big deal. But the twins hadn't been at the Pixel Comics booth—Fi had missed the end of the signing by minutes. And she couldn't go back toward the AC Comics booth for fear of James M. And so she just started . . . running, to every corner of the con, ignoring texts from her parents, in the hopes that she might find her siblings. And the worst part about it?

She was now . . .

As sweaty and smelly . . .

As everyone. Else. Here.

Fi finally slowed to a brisk walk in one of the more sparsely populated areas of the con and decided to just accept it. This was her life now. She lived here. She lived here in this nerd convention surrounded by smelly nerds and would just slowly become one of them. It was inevitable.

But, Fi wondered to herself, slowing her pace even further . . . was it that bad? She thought about Rowan again and swallowed.

Rowan was a nerd. And she smelled *great*.

How did she even manage that in here? Fi made a mental note to ask her later.

If Fi ever managed to find her again. *Ugh.*

All hope lost, Fi decided to stop looking into the faces of the people around her for her siblings and to *start* looking at where she was. She found herself in a couple of rows that a giant ceiling-hung sign identified as ARTIST ALLEY. This looked different from the rest of the con, Fi noticed; there was no corporate branding or flashy TVs, no gigantic lines or people in branded T-shirts trying desperately to shove a free bookmark in your face. Instead, there were rows upon rows of individual tables set up like a craft fair, each booth with its own unique flair. And so many of the people sitting behind the tables, Fi noticed, were super-stylish young women. They were selling prints and original sketches and pins and stickers; that one had *Lunar Soldier*–themed art, but all the characters were dressed like cool tattooed biker babes; this one had a ton of *Vigilante League* art, but the boy Vigilante Leaguers were smooching. *Cute.*

"Here, you can have a card!" said the girl behind the *Vigilante League* booth. She couldn't have been that much older than Fi.

"Oh, thanks," Fi said, grabbing the business card from the girl's outstretched hand. The card had all the artist's social media info on it.

"No problem. You a *Vigilante League* fan?" she asked, tucking a long strand of purple-tipped black hair behind her ear.

"Not really?" Fi answered. "I was just admiring the art."

"Thanks." The girl smiled. "This is my full-time job now, so I'm always happy when people dig it."

Fi just goggled at the girl. "This is your *job*?"

"Yeah." The artist laughed. "I can't believe it either, most days. But I travel to a lot of shows and put out a lot of new merch all the time. I feel equal parts lucky and exhausted."

"That's so cool," Fi said, and really meant it.

"Seriously, thanks. Find me online!" The girl waved, sitting back down at her table. "We can stay in touch. The best part of the con!"

Fi nodded and tucked the girl's card into her back jeans pocket. Between that girl and Rowan . . . Fi was starting to understand what people found so appealing about all this. Just a little bit, anyway. People could really, genuinely celebrate the things they loved. And they could do it together.

Her phone dinged again, bringing Fi back down to Earth. She opened her texts—her mom. *Again.* Thank goodness she didn't have read receipts turned on. Fi knew she would have to answer them soon, or they were going to think she'd died somewhere on the con floor.

Mamička: are you having fun

Mamička: are the twins having fun

Mamička: are the twins with you

Mamička: is Alex engaging

Mamička: Fiorella answer me

Mamička: I hope you are in line for something very good right now

Mamička: we will talk about your phone habits later

Mamička: I think I just saw Criss Angel

And so on and so forth for hours. She was still going to be toast if she couldn't find the twins. She was—

"Guess who?!" Fi's whole world went dark in an instant. Someone was covering her eyes from behind. Was it Cat?! No, she wasn't that tall yet (thankfully). Fi took a deep breath and her heart sped up—and she grabbed at the hands on her face.

"Rowan!" Fi ducked and spun, keeping her hold on Rowan's hands. They wrestled for a second before Fi broke free and punched Rowan's shoulder.

"Ow, you're strong!" She laughed.

"I'm a jock," Fi explained.

"Are you also from the eighties?" Rowan laughed even harder.

"Shut *up*." Fi punched Rowan again playfully, even though she wanted the exact opposite. "How'd you find me?"

"I just looked for the person who stood out most in the crowd," Rowan said with a smirk.

Fi, still a little red from her interaction with the cool artist, flushed harder. She spent her whole life trying to fit in. Was *she* really the weirdo here?

"At least I'm not a big nerd," Fi said half-heartedly.

"Your loss, dude." Rowan shrugged. "No luck on the twins front, I take it?"

Fi shook her head. "They're monsters. It's hopeless."

"It's never hopeless," Rowan encouraged. "Superhero movies taught me that. You've got to keep your chin up."

"You have no idea what you're talking about," Fi said. "My parents are going to kill me. I'm totally screwed. Just let me be angry at the twins for five seconds, here."

"Are you sure you're angry at the twins?" Rowan asked pointedly.

Fi blinked. She had never felt more confused about who she was or what she wanted or what she was supposed to be doing. She was angry at the twins but grateful she wasn't alone; frustrated to be at the convention but kind of on a weird adventure now; missing her friends but admittedly sorta kinda enjoying Rowan's company, too. There was just a lot going on in her head.

And Rowan was right; it wasn't all about the twins. Not anymore.

"I don't know." Fi sighed. "Let's check social one more time."

Both Fi and Rowan hopped onto their phones, scrolling through every app, hashtag, and account they could think of. Life-sized animal cosplayer . . . huge crowd . . . TV show panel . . . definitely Criss Angel . . .

Fi looked over at Rowan's phone and grabbed her thumb before she could keep scrolling. "Wait, there!"

"There?" Rowan asked, centering the previous pic.

"There!" Fi said excitedly. It was a photo of a gigantic line outside—it looked like it went on for miles. People had lawn chairs and sleeping bags even. And there, toward the very back of the line, was Cat's unmistakable blue hair.

"That's the Hall M line!" Rowan said excitedly. "And this was just posted a minute ago!"

Fi was already running.

"You don't know where you're going!" Rowan said with a laugh, bypassing her.

"You take the lead!" Fi answered.

But she didn't slow down.

19

Cat was totally flabbergasted. She did not know how to spell that word, but she definitely knew how to say it and what it meant. And that was what she was feeling at that exact moment.

Alex had *abandoned* her. In her time of *need*. She'd basically been the one moving this Quest thing forward the whole day—she'd even been willing to break the rules to win!—and all it'd gotten her were lost Hall M passes and an angry brother. And an empty stomach. Eating healthy at a convention was so, so hard.

Cat tugged at one of her loafers, adjusting the heel so it stopped rubbing on her fresh blister. She shifted her weight to her other foot—and adjusted her other loafer, because of *another* blister. These decoupaged shoes were going to be the end of her, Cat knew it.

Well, blisters or no, she didn't need Alex, Cat decided. She could do this *without* him. She *could* and *would* win the Quest alone. Help was for the *weak*. Brothers were *jerks*. She could do this. She was in the *right*.

Right?

She would just have to take matters into her own hands. If she didn't have a pass, she'd get into Hall M like everyone else. It was easy. All she had to do was brave the line.

The gigantic line.

That people sometimes spent full days in. And slept overnight in.

And she was definitely, absolutely at the very end of it.

This is fine! Cat repeated over and over in her head, hopping from one foot to the other, wincing away in her pain. *Totally fine! For absolutely sure!*

Car tried to count the number of people in front of her in line. One, two, three, six, six hundred, sixteen thousand . . . yep, definitely about sixteen thousand million, no question. Then she tried to count the seconds until the line started moving. One locomotive, two locomotive, three, oh, Dark Spider, she was *so bored* and there was *nothing for her to do and no one for her to talk to!*

Cat flopped down on the cold ground, taking the pressure off her aching heels, and eyed the blankets and chairs of the folks around her with great jealousy. Alex probably would have thought to bring a cushion.

Minutes ticked by.

Then more minutes.

Then still.

More.

Minutes.

This was taking . . .

Forever.

After easily at least ten hours (*how had it only been fifteen minutes?!*), Cat stood up to stretch her legs.

"Catalina Gallo!" she heard a voice bellow.

Cat immediately crouched down again. She knew that voice. It was scarier than even James M. It was . . .

"*There* you are!" Her sister Fi's head popped around the person standing in line in front of her. Fi hopped over the barrier keeping people from cutting into line without so much as a second thought.

Cat sighed. She supposed getting caught by Fi

was pretty much the least of her worries at this point.

But she wasn't standing up. Her heels were in too much pain for that.

"Your sister?" a new voice asked. Cat looked up and saw someone following Fi into line. She had shaggy purple hair, dark roots artfully showing through near her scalp. (Though Fi's friend looked like she could be a boy *or* a girl—or both or neither!—Cat took her cue from the SHE/HER! pronoun sticker hanging off the bottom of the badge around her neck.) Cat was surprised but also stoked to see the girl was wearing *Voltage: Defenders of Legend* leggings. What was someone so obviously cool doing hanging out with her sister?

"Are those Jess Carrell pins?" Cat had noticed the rainbow of happily violent pins affixed to the girl's denim vest and scrambled to her feet to get a better look. Now *this* was worth suffering through blister pain for.

"'Oh, hello, older sister; sorry I put you through a living nightmare today and forced you to run through nerdtopia for literal hours in order to find me.'" Cat heard Fi's sarcasm but was too busy examining pins. She was dying for that one with the pink cat holding the spiky baseball bat. It was a mood.

The purple-haired girl laughed. "Jess Carrell's stuff is the best," she confirmed. She stuck her hand out, forcing Cat to take a step back in order to shake it properly like a cool adult or whatever. "I'm Rowan; you must be Cat."

Cat went to grasp Rowan's outstretched hand but opted at the last minute to go for a sideways high five instead. Always keep 'em guessing.

"That's me," she replied. "Do I know you?" The more Cat stared at the girl, the more familiar she looked. Was it the purple hair . . . ? Cat could have sworn she'd seen her before, though she had no idea where. Maybe in line somewhere . . . ?

"Nope!" the girl responded cheerfully, pushing a hand through her bangs. "But I've been helping Fi look for you. She's been worried, like . . . a *lot*, dude."

Cat took a deep breath—she'd have to get it over with sometime, so it might as well be now, right?—and turned to face her sister. Fi had been standing to the side, watching this whole thing between Cat and Rowan go down in silence. Fi's face was a fun shade of purple that Cat didn't know the name for. She'd have to look it up later.

"Hiiiiiiii, Fi." Cat plastered her sweetest smile onto her face, holding her hands under her chin and batting her eyes. "Have you been having the best time?"

The purple got a little darker. Maybe that had been the wrong approach? Should Cat have just made a break for it instead? But she was stuck here in this line—

"Have I . . . been having . . . fun?" Fi interrupted Cat's thoughts when she started speaking, each word increasing in volume. "Rowan." Fi turned to the other girl, her eyes taking on a wild vibe that Cat was definitely not into. "Would you say I've been having *fun*?!"

Rowan, to her credit, looked like she'd rather be anywhere else in that moment than between Cat and her older sister, who was definitely, absolutely coming loose at the seams. "Well, uh." Rowan swallowed. "I kinda hoped you'd been having a good—"

"That's not the point!" Fi exploded. The people napping on the blankets in front of them jolted awake with a start. Whoops. "Do you have any idea what I've been through today?! What were you *thinking*?! And *where*," Fi added, breathing heavily, "is our *brother*?!"

Cat crossed her arms across her chest. How *dare* Fi even ask her about Alex right now. "You're not the only one who's been through some stuff today—" Cat began defensively.

"You are in *no* position to be snarky with me right now!" Fi cut Cat off before she could even finish her thought.

"You don't understand—"

"You're right!" Fi cut Cat off *again*. "And I don't want to! We're leaving!"

Leaving?! "We can't!" Cat said quickly. "We have to—"

"We have to *find Mom and Dad*!" Why wouldn't Fi let Cat finish a single thought?!

"If you'd just *listen*—"

"We're *out*," Fi interrupted, *again*, like it was final. Even as Fi started to march out of line, Cat just stood there, fuming. She felt like she was going to burst into tears and she never, ever, positively *ever* cried where other people could see her. She spent *way* too long on her eyeliner for that! How could Fi not even let her get a word in edgewise? How could Fi not let Cat explain what was going on here? Why this was important? How could Fi be . . . ?

Telling her what to do.

Cat blinked.

Oh.

Oh.

Cat's breath caught in her throat and she plunked back down onto the ground, ignoring her sister's yelling. Cat dropped her head into her hands and started counting slowly to ten, which always seemed to work for Alex.

Alex. Is this how he'd been feeling while Cat had been directing their moves for the Quest? She hadn't *meant* to be insensitive or thoughtless— she was just trying to be efficient and get stuff done. Sometimes Alex was too quiet and unsure for his own good, you know? But, Cat realized, that didn't matter. As much as they were participating in the Quest to win, they were also doing it because they *loved* doing it. *Together.* Being in charge didn't have to mean controlling everything. Alex just wanted to be treated like a partner, not a sidekick. Why hadn't Cat been able to see that sooner? Before everything had fallen apart?

Reaching the count of ten, Cat took a deep breath and found she could fill her lungs again. She took her hands away from her face and saw Fi stomping back over to her spot in the line.

Cat didn't know what she was supposed to do now. Leave with Fi? Give up the Quest?

But was the Quest even worth it without Alex?

"Catalina—"

"Wait!" Rowan, who had been following Cat's sister, skidded between the two siblings. "Fi, seriously, wait." Rowan put her hand on Fi's shoulder. To Cat's great surprise, she thought she saw her sister actually *blush*.

Cat stopped herself from rolling her eyes. Crushes were gross, but they might actually help her out, just this one time.

"Rowan, we have got to get back to my parents—"

"Fine." Rowan threw her hands out, exasperated. "That's fine. You'll get your *camping*." Cat thought she heard a note of disdain in the girl's voice.

"My what—?" Fi sounded confused, but Rowan didn't let her finish.

"But Alex isn't *here*. We've got to find him first. Okay?"

Fi nodded. "That's what I'm trying to say."

"Good." Rowan squeezed Fi's shoulder and turned back to Cat. "Now. Where's your brother?"

20

Alex had never felt so lost in his life.

Not *literally*. He had the GeekiCon map and schedule memorized weeks earlier. He'd been to this convention a million times before. He knew exactly where he was and where he was going.

But he also had *no idea* where he was going. He was just . . . going.

Alex trudged around the upper floor of the con, passing by lines for panel rooms, lines for bathrooms, lines for food vendors, lines for signings . . . Now that he thought about it, GeekiCon really was a lot of lines.

At least they kept the people organized and out of Alex's way. For the most part.

As he wandered the con's packed corridors, Alex stared at his feet and tried to keep his breathing steady. Right, left. In, out. Right, then left. In, then out.

Alex found his way to a small open space against a wall and put his back to it, sliding down to the floor. He pulled his game console out of his bag and powered it on. He would just sit here and play until the day ended. That was fine, right? He did that at home all the time. Hours would go by in a flash. No big deal.

But Alex couldn't focus on his screen. Every time he tried to concentrate on his game, his eyes went blurry. There wasn't anything physically wrong with him, he was pretty sure—he was just so *distracted*.

Every time he tried to stop being angry at Cat, he just *couldn't*. She had completely ruined this day. Everything had been going so *great*. If she'd just . . . not been so inconsiderate, and not cheated, and not given away their passes, and— and . . .

Alex let out a frustrated sigh and stuffed his console back into his messenger bag. He looked up at the con-goers passing by in front of him instead, hoping the colors and the crowds would take his mind off things. There was a family all cosplaying the Impossibles; over in line, someone had dressed up their service dog like the star of the latest season of *The Biting Dead*; ascending the big escalators were a group of people laughing as one of their capes got stuck under their spiky heel.

"Okay, c'mon; we only have a minute and then we gotta go!" someone yelled over the din of the crowd. Alex looked to his left, where a big group of women, all dressed like different iterations of the warrior queen from *Star Worlds*, was gathered. They were taking a crew photo, and they all had their biceps flexed like that lady from that old poster about girls being able to do anything including make bombs and stuff.

Alex actually found himself smiling. General Queen Lara was his favorite *Star Worlds* character. The actress who played her in the original films from the '70s had died just recently, and there were a ton of people cosplaying as Lara in her honor. Even, Alex noticed, his grin widening, some guys.

"No fear!" one of the cosplayers shouted.

"No fear!" the rest shouted back in unison. "Only the Power!"

It was Lara's most famous phrase from the film. "The Power" was a magical invisible force in the movies that connected all people and things to one another (and also gave people cool telekinesis and precognition and brain-controlled swords). Alex knew, of course, that the Power was actually a metaphor for love and for believing in yourself and in others and all the rest of that good, touchy-feely stuff. Lara had the most power of anyone in the *Star Worlds* universe, and she had sacrificed herself to save the resistance.

Alex felt his anger melting away as he watched the Laras chant and pose in front of the vast number of cell phones attached to humans who had assembled to capture the moment. Alex remembered Lara's calm demeanor in the face of great obstacles. Even when her own planet exploded, Lara managed to keep it together. She didn't blame anyone else for her problems. She just *dealt* with them.

Was Alex being unfair, blaming his sister for everything that had gone wrong with the Quest today? Sure, she had done some really ridiculous stuff. And she'd suffered some serious consequences for them.

But, Alex thought with another big sigh, she hadn't been totally off the mark. He really *did* struggle to stand up for himself sometimes. He liked having Cat's help with things like crowds and big social situations. And he hadn't been as involved with planning out Quest items before the con as he could have been. As much as he hated to admit it, Alex realized he couldn't entirely blame Cat for feeling like she had to take control of the situation. He wished she'd gone about it differently, sure. But he also could have spoken up sooner and more productively. Like General Queen Lara.

The group of cosplayers was breaking up, each of the Laras going their separate ways. Alex looked at his calculator watch. It wasn't too late. If he could just find his sister . . . there was still time. Alex braced his hands on the floor next to him (and made a mental note to use hand sanitizer ASAP) and pushed himself to his feet.

No fear, Alex repeated to himself. *Only the Power.*

He stepped forward toward the escalator—

And walked right into someone.

"Oh, sorry—" Alex mumbled, pushing back off the guy's chest. Alex clearly wasn't the one at fault, but he still felt the need to apologize, even when someone else had stopped right in front of *him*. Maybe because his dad was Minnesotan.

"You're about to be," the man responded. Alex, his balance recovered, looked up.

Right into James M.'s scowling face.

"You must have the wrong person—" Alex tried to channel Cat but was never quite as convincing as his sister could be.

"Oh no." James M. laughed, crossing his arms over his sweat-stained T-shirt. "Where's your sister? Or did she have the good sense to go back to her online echo chamber?"

"I have no idea what you're talking about—" Alex looked around frantically for a way out, but James M. had him trapped between his body and the wall. There was nowhere to run, and no one at the con was going to dare question someone with a CON STAFF badge. Alex was trapped!

"Well, one of you Questies is better than none." James M. shrugged, grabbing Alex by the back of his neck. Alex shuddered—he hated being touched without being asked first and *especially* hated being touched by *strangers*.

"Get *off*—" Alex clawed at James M.'s clammy hand, which just gripped him tighter.

"I don't think so," James M. snapped, pulling Alex toward the down escalator. "Every one of you who gets kicked out of my con for life is another fake nerd Questie SJW I never have to see again."

"It's not *your con*!" Alex shot back, dragging

his feet onto the moving step. James M. was so much bigger than him, and Alex wasn't exactly a varsity athlete like Fi. He didn't know what else to do but be dragged along. It wasn't like he could have jumped off the escalator, anyway. Was he really about to be banned from GeekiCon for *life*?!

What was he going to do?!

And what was he going to tell *Cat*?!

21

Fi was being dragged back into the convention center by her younger sister, their hands sweaty from the sweltering midafternoon heat. Cat had given up her spot in the Hall M line to the person behind her when they bolted. That line was outside the actual convention center, with long-suffering line standers protected from the sun by a series of canopies and umbrellas.

Even though Fi was getting the hang of this whole convention thing, she still couldn't really understand what would drive someone to sleep in line for days just to sit in the middle of a gigantic panel room and watch a TV star through a pair of binoculars. But maybe she just hadn't leveled up to that extreme yet. At the very least, Fi thought, it explained some of the grosser smells in the convention center.

Fi's other hand clutched Rowan, who was being dragged along behind *her*. They were like a panicked human daisy chain led by a twelve-year-old with blue-tipped hair. What could possibly go wrong?

"Fi!" she heard Rowan call out from behind her. Not letting go of Cat's hand—she was *not* losing this kid again—Fi craned her neck around to glance at Rowan.

Rowan gave her a thumbs-up with her free hand. She was grinning from ear to ear. "We got this!"

Fi laughed, almost tripping over herself as Cat tugged her forward with more strength than she thought her younger sister had. "Okay!"

The three of them flew past the same glass double doors through which the Gallo family had entered GeekiCon in a similar rush this morning, each of them slapping their passes against the scanners without needing to be reminded. Cat hopped on the escalator to their right, the huge one that took them up through the atrium to the convention center's second level.

"This way!" Cat shouted back at Fi and Rowan. "I think Alex'll be hiding upstairs!"

Fi jumped onto the escalator, tugging Rowan onto the step behind her. Rowan put her arms around Fi's waist, breathing heavily, and rested her head against Fi's back. Fi could feel Rowan's laughter in her very bones. Fi couldn't help but laugh back. Did she ever imagine she'd find herself in a situation like this?

"Cat!" Fi heard someone yell. The three girls looked around frantically.

"Alex!" Cat shouted back, jumping up and down on the escalator step. "Fi, there!"

Fi followed the trajectory of her sister's outstretched arm. She was pointing to the descending escalator next to them. There, at the top, was Alex, slowly making his way downward, waving his arms around like a drowning monkey.

And behind him, his hand gripping the back of Alex's neck, was James M., talking into his phone and ignoring his captive's shouts.

"*That* creep!" Rowan said, untangling herself from around Fi's back and grabbing on to the escalator's handrail.

"You know him?!" Cat whipped around,

looking at Fi and Rowan with surprise. "He's been after us all day!"

"Us, too!" Fi responded.

"He wants to ban everyone playing the Quest," Cat explained in a hurry.

"And everyone he doesn't think lives up to what a geek is *supposed* to be," confirmed Rowan, spitting the words out with contempt.

"Yeah, he's the worst," Fi agreed. But he had Alex. The groups were about to pass each other on the escalators, one going up and one going down. They were running out of time. How were they going to save him?

"Fi," Rowan said, twisting around to look at her, "item eighteen!"

That was it. *That was it!*

"Rowan, you're a genius," Fi said, ripping her drawstring backpack off and tugging out the soccer ball she always had on her.

Now, just like they did for Quest item eighteen—play a sport on the main escalators—Fi bounced the ball from knee to knee, getting a bit of momentum going. The people in front of and behind her leaned away and complained nervously, but she didn't care. Fi kneed the ball as high as she could get it, clutching the handrail with one hand to keep her balance. Launching herself upward, Fi slammed the ball with her forehead with as much force as she could muster in the limited amount of space she had. Also, without falling to her doom.

The ball flew forward, straight toward James M.'s face.

Human reflexes are a funny thing, Fi thought, as she watched the whole thing go down almost in slow motion. Even the most unathletic person in the world really wants to avoid a high-speed soccer ball to the face. And sure enough, desperate to avoid a broken nose, James M.'s arms flew up to guard his face.

Which, of course, meant he had let go of Alex.

"I've got you!" Fi yelled across the escalator railings. "Do it!"

Fi could see the hesitation on her brother's face—but only for a second. Alex knew she would never let him down.

And she wouldn't.

Alex planted both of his hands firmly on the handrail separating the up from the down side of the escalator and vaulted his legs across. *Good thing he's so scrawny*, Fi thought wildly, reaching out her arms to catch Alex as he leaped from one escalator to the other. Fi grabbed Alex by the waist and hefted him the rest of the way over.

Shocked that she'd managed to keep her balance on a moving escalator through all this, Fi realized belatedly that Rowan had wrapped one arm around her waist and was firmly grasping the outside handrail with the other.

Cat swooped in the second Alex's feet were firmly on the up escalator. She paused long enough to see him nod before throwing her arms around his shoulders. Fi wondered how her high-pitched "*squeeee!*" must have sounded that close to Alex's ear.

"I'll find you!" James M. bellowed. Fi spun around to see him still descending on his side of the escalator. He was holding her soccer ball in his hands.

And he looked *furious*.

"Go, go, go!" Fi shouted to her little pack of nerds, urging them forward. She started taking the escalator up two steps at a time, belatedly apologizing to the other con-goers she had to inelegantly shove out of the way in the process. They were going to make this. They *were*.

"'Scuse us; coming through. Thanks so much!"

22

Cat wheezed, pumping her arms hard as she bolted through the con. After Fi had launched her soccer ball at James M.'s head (very awesome!!) and Alex had essentially hurdled over the famous GeekiCon escalators (extremely double awesome, what the heck!!!), Cat had felt Fi's hand shove into the small of her back and knew it was time to get moving. Cat took the moving steps as fast as she could—though normally she would never walk up an escalator, just on principle. (Its literal whole job is to do the walking for you; what is even the point?) When she reached the second floor, Cat just kept running, trusting that the rest of her family—and Rowan—would be with her.

Cat's lungs were about to burst out of her chest like the alien in that one scary movie with the buff space lady that she definitely was not allowed to watch but had streamed online anyway one time and had nightmares for weeks because of it. Fi was the soccer player; she was the runner in the family. Cat wasn't exactly Alex—she liked to go to the climbing gym with her parents sometimes and really enjoyed dodgeball day in PE—but, and she was being completely, totally honest with herself here, she was not made for distance activities.

But escaping James M., it turned out, was the exact motivation Cat needed to become a runner.

But run to where?! Cat thought in a panic, her breath coming in short puffs as she raced down the emptiest corridor she could find. If James M. got off at the bottom of the escalator and hopped right back on again, he'd be on their trail at any moment. They had to find a place to *hide*.

Cat made a sharp turn down another hallway, this one even less populated than the last. Without even slowing down, she grabbed the nearest panel-room door she could find and swung it open, rushing through. The panel must have been something pretty small-time—there were a few speakers up front and only about fifteen audience members in the room. Cat skidded down the empty back row of seats and threw herself into the very last one. A couple of people had turned around to look at her funny, but mostly she was being ignored. She'd done it!

. . . That is, until Fi, Rowan, and Alex blasted through the door behind her, causing such a ruckus that the panelists actually stopped talking for a second to figure out what was going on.

"Sorry!" Cat gasped out, waving one of her arms from her seat and still struggling to catch her breath. "So sorry! We just realized we were late and didn't want to miss the rest of the panel. We so totally, absolutely love you guys," she added, hoping they would fall for a little flattery. It was Cat's favorite get-out-of-trouble trick. Cat had no clue who they were, but they seemed nice, so it was probably fine.

Alex dropped into the seat next to her, wheezing. Rowan just sat right down on the floor in front of the chairs, her purple bangs sticking to her sweaty forehead. Fi, of course, was just lightly glowing. Her breathing was totally fine.

Show-off.

"What are we—?" Fi started to talk, but Rowan held up a hand to stop her. Fi shut up for a second while everyone else just breathed heavily for a couple of seconds and collected themselves. Cat tossed her hair into a quick ponytail to get it off the back of her neck and gave her sister a nod.

"What are we going to do?" Fi hissed, trying to keep her voice down so as not to disturb the panelists at the front of the room.

"'We'?" Cat whispered back. "What do you mean 'we'?"

"Fi's been collecting Quest items for you!" Rowan said, her voice muted but proud. "Didn't you wonder who was crossing things off your list?"

Alex just nodded. Cat could see the gears in his head turning as he put it all together. "You're our GeekiCon angel. That's how you knew what item eighteen was."

"Playing sports on the escalators," Fi whispered back with a grin. "Twice in one day!"

"Shh!" One of the other audience members turned around to hush them. Cat put up her hands in an apologetic gesture until the person turned around again. They had a really tall hat on that had to be part of a costume, but Cat had no idea for what. There were a *lot* of fandoms out there; it was hard, sometimes, to keep up.

"You don't have many items left," Rowan said, lowering her voice even further so as not to risk disturbing the panel again. "I think, if we split up, you could get it done."

"And we'll be harder for James M. to catch if we're apart," Fi added.

Cat shook her head. "First of all, it's totally weird that you're into this all of a sudden," she whispered to Fi, who just shrugged. "But also, it's supercool and so I can't blame you and I'm just glad that you're finally admitting that being a nerd is awesome—no take backs, I said what I said."

Fi pursed her lips but didn't argue. *For once!*

"But we can't get into Hall M," Alex added, keeping his voice low, too. "We lost our passes."

"*I* gave away our passes," Cat corrected. It was time to be a big kid and take responsibility for her goof-up. She turned to Alex and looked him in the eye, even though she knew he would probably look away in a couple of seconds. "I'm sorry, Alex. I totally—"

"*Shhhhh!*"

"Sorry!" Cat and her crew all leaned their heads closer together. "Seriously, Alex, I totally screwed up. I should have been a better listener. Some of the best parts of the day today were the unplanned things you stumbled into." Cat bit her lip. "I really did just want to win for both of us."

"It's okay," Alex said, giving Cat a small smile. He tucked his chin down but kept talking. "Without your plans, we wouldn't have gotten nearly as many Quest items done. I shouldn't have gotten upset with you for taking charge, and I should have been more patient. I could have done a lot more and I just didn't."

"It probably would have helped if I'd listened to you guys, like, even one time," Fi added. Rowan squeezed her hand and Fi smiled at her before continuing. "All I could think about was my camping trip and not what any of this meant to you both."

"I literally just met all of you dudes like thirty seconds ago, but Fi's really rad and I'm glad everyone seems to be getting along now," Rowan added quickly.

Cat had to stifle a laugh. Rowan seemed way cool, actually.

"Yeah, well." Cat tossed her ponytail back and forth. "We're family."

"Selfie!" Rowan said, holding up her camera to capture a picture of the four of them. They shoved together and she hit the shutter—and the flash went off. *Sound and all.*

The panelists stood up, and the volunteer guarding the door was on Cat and the crew in seconds. Laughing harder than she probably should have been, Cat let herself be ushered out of the room behind Rowan, Fi, and Alex.

Back out in the hallway, Cat stood next to the door and huddled up with her fam. Rowan showed the others the selfie on her phone (completely cute, thanks!), but the screen was interrupted by an alert.

"Oh My Academic Heroine! . . . 'New Quest Item Added'?" Cat read off the screen. She felt her heart start pounding almost as hard as it had been when they'd gotten to this room in the first place. "Is that for real?!"

23

Alex snatched his phone out of his messenger bag and had the Quest app open before Cat could even finish asking her question. It wasn't unheard of for the Quest to add random items over the course of the day; they were usually small challenges to keep people checking the app and on their toes. Really, Corwin Blake was kind of a prankster online. He did all this for charity, but it was widely speculated that he also did it because he had a really messed-up sense of humor and enjoyed watching people do ridiculous things in service of his goals.

But mostly the charity thing. Probably.

There it was: "New Quest Item Added!" Alex

clicked on the notifications tab and checked the list.

"Look!" Alex said, flipping his phone around so everyone could see it. Sure enough, there at the bottom of the list, Corwin had added a special task just moments ago. All the item said was "Find this." When Alex clicked the item, it took him to a blurry photo with absolutely no context around it.

Just . . . a blurry photo.

"Find that?!" Cat burst out. "How?!"

"What is it?" Fi asked, equally confused.

"Check the list again," Rowan suggested. "Does it say anything else?"

Alex flipped the phone back around. He frowned as he scrolled up and down, hoping for any little hidden hint they might find. "Nothing."

"Wait, here!" Rowan jabbed her finger at her own phone. "Look—the Rewards page!"

Alex quickly popped over to that section of the app. This was where it detailed what you got if your team managed to get the most points in the Quest: spending a week with Corwin and his *Paranormal* costars doing charity work and the chance to qualify for a special mentorship. Cat cared about the celebs (and the charity work, if Alex was being fair). Alex cared about the mentorship. He really wanted to know how he could get to the next level with his art.

But there! Rowan was right. At the very bottom of the page, there was something new, in teeny-tiny font, that hadn't been there before. Alex squinted at his screen and read the text out loud.

"The first Quest participants to successfully upload a photo of the Surprise Mystery Item will win a Surprise Mystery Prize to be presented at the Quest Masquerade Awards Banquet this evening. Good luck, Questers!"

"Cool," Fi admitted, almost without realizing it. Rowan stuck her tongue out at her.

"It's not just cool," the purple-haired gal corrected. "It's *epic*."

"It's just a blurry picture!" Cat wailed in despair. "How can we find this *and* find our way into Hall M?!"

"Fi's right," Rowan said, tucking her phone away. "The best way to get everything done—and to avoid that complete toolbag James M.—is to split up."

Alex couldn't help but agree. He didn't like many people without getting to know them first, but Alex was starting to think Rowan might be someone he could like. Eventually. "Who wants to go where?"

"I'm sticking with Alex," Cat said firmly. Alex looked at her with surprise—he supposed they were okay again, after all that.

"Sounds good," Alex agreed, giving his sister a smile back. They were always okay again. That was the best thing about being twins with Cat.

"Obviously." Fi rolled her eyes. "But who's taking the Surprise Mystery Item?"

"We can do that," Rowan volunteered. "I know the con pretty well. I'm sure we can find it."

Alex nodded. "And we can get into Hall M."

"Cocky, but making it fashion," Rowan said approvingly. Alex didn't know what that meant, but it sounded positive. "I dig it. Text when you're done, okay?"

"Not if we text them first!" Fi laughed. She grabbed Rowan's hand, and the two of them split, running back toward the escalators.

"Don't get kicked out of the con for life!" Cat called after them. She shook her head and shrugged at Alex once they were out of earshot. "Teenagers."

"So weird," Alex agreed. "And I'm probably the weirdest one here, so I can say that."

"If you're the weirdest, then I'm the weirdinator," Cat said firmly. Alex didn't know what that meant, either, but that was pretty typical for a

Cat-ism. "Still. I think it's good we're doing Hall M. I feel like . . . it's our *destiny* now, you know?"

"I think so, too," Alex agreed. "We can do it. I know we can do it."

"I know we can do it, too." Cat smiled. Alex could see his sister struggling to keep the smile on her face.

"What is it?" Alex pressed.

Cat sighed. "It's just . . ." She dropped her head down and stared at the floor. "I have no idea how we're going to get in. I know we're being all cool about it now but . . . I really did give away our passes. And the line is ten trillion miles long. We have no chance of making it in there by the end of the day."

"Oh." Alex laughed. "That's it?"

Cat stared at him like he'd grown another head and *that* head had seven ears and one of them was maybe purple. "Yeah," she said. "That's pretty big."

Alex grinned. "When I said I know we can do it, I was being serious. This time, I really *did* plan ahead. Follow me!"

Alex took off in the same direction as Rowan and Fi. Cat kept pace at his side.

"Where are we going?" she asked excitedly.

"It's a surprise!"

"Why?"

"Because . . . surprises are fun?" Alex suggested.

Cat laughed. "You surprise me all the time, bud."

Alex and Cat reached the escalators and took one down, peeking out over the sides for any sign of James M. It looked like the coast was clear—for now. Alex couldn't believe they'd managed to lose him. He could still feel James M.'s clammy phantom hands on the back of his neck. Alex shuddered.

Thinking about James M. just intensified Alex's desire to see this Quest item through to the end. If James M. thought they weren't real nerds—well, Alex would show him. He would show everybody who ever doubted him!

"This way!" Alex said, scanning his pass and bursting out the double doors into the sunshine.

"I believe in you!" Cat sounded like she was trying really hard to convince herself of that. It was okay—Alex knew he was on the right track. For both of them.

Alex led Cat down, down, down the convention center's long outdoor veranda. He rounded the concrete corner. There, across the way, was the press hotel. Over there was the Hall M line—as gigantic as Cat said it was. There was the sound of the ocean, just on the other side of the building . . .

And *there* was the press door to Hall M.

Still completely unguarded.

Alex couldn't believe his luck. He'd hoped on the great Adrianna Tack that it would still be here waiting for him when he returned with Cat. And here it was. Alex sent up a silent *thank-you* to his idol (it was ridiculous, but just in case) and started toward it.

"Wait . . . ," Cat said, clearly processing what was happening. "Are we . . . ?"

"We are," Alex said firmly. "Because sometimes . . ."

Alex reached out and grabbed the handle. He swallowed. He squeezed the lever.

Click.

Still completely unlocked.

Alex cracked the door open and jerked his head, indicating that Cat should go in first. She slid through the small crack, and Alex snuck in behind her, shutting it silently behind them. They were in the little blocked-off antechamber Alex had found last time. Through the black curtains in front of them, Alex could hear the muted sounds of whatever gigantic panel was taking place in Hall M at the moment. He thought for a second. At this time . . . probably *The Heroes of Justice*. Cat was just staring at Alex with her mouth wide open. He loved when she was shocked into silence. It happened so rarely!

Alex grinned back at Cat. He whispered, finishing his thought from a moment ago. "Sometimes, one really *does* simply walk in the back door."

24

"Do you think they made it into Hall M?" Fi was speedwalking the floor with Rowan, desperately searching for that Special Mystery Super Bonus Item Extravaganza.

"Between us?" Rowan responded, getting up on her tiptoes to peek at something on a booth's upper level. She shook her head and kept power walking. Guess that wasn't it. "I don't know. It's famously impossible to get into Hall M without a pass or, you know, sleeping in line for days."

"If anyone can do it, it's them," Fi said with as much confidence as she could muster. "I mean, I hope so," she added after a moment. "I've been ignoring my mom's texts all day on the off chance that they can. So they better."

"What does that mean for your camping trip?" Rowan asked casually, turning down another aisle as quickly as the con crowds would allow it.

"I . . ." Fi started to speak but stopped herself just as quickly. What *did* this mean for her camping trip? There's no way her mom wasn't going to be furious with her after this whole fiasco. And a furious Mom meant no definitely, totally chaperoned weekend away with all the coolest kids in her grade.

But also . . . did she care? Was that something she even cared about anymore? Fi slowed her pace to examine her surroundings more carefully. She'd been so afraid to be seen at this convention because of what Ethan and their friends—well, *his* friends, really—might think of her. But, Fi realized, she'd never bothered to think about what *she* thought of *them*.

Yes, obviously everyone was obsessed with them and wanted to be tagged in their party pics online. But did Fi want to be in those photos because being at those parties would actually make her happy? Every time she hung around Ethan, Fi felt like she was putting on a mask—one way less colorful and awesome than the ones here at the convention. She felt like she always had to pretend to be someone she wasn't, and that—at any moment—Ethan and his friends would realize she wasn't cool enough to be around them and they would kick her out of their cool kid gang forever.

But Fi hadn't felt that way around Rowan. Not even one time. Maybe it was because Fi *honestly* hadn't cared about what Rowan thought about her at all when they first met. And despite that, Rowan *still* seemed to like her and wanted to spend time with her. Fi was even, somehow, having fun at GeekiCon.

At *GeekiCon*!

Her mom might ground Fi for all eternity, but at least she'd be excited to hear *that*.

"You what?" Rowan asked, nudging Fi in the side. Fi realized she hadn't finished her sentence.

Instead, Fi spun around to face Rowan and grabbed the girl's hands. "Over here." She looked around quickly and saw a side of the *Lunar Soldier* booth nearby. The employees had set up a makeshift shop with lots of different comics and collectables, and it was filled with people milling around. Perfect.

She tugged Rowan over, through the window-shopping crowd, and tucked herself into an empty corner. No one was paying attention to them in the midst of all this *Lunar Soldier* excitement. Was Fi going to have to actually watch this show after the con was over?

Maybe.

Rowan pulled her phone out of her pocket, probably to open the Quest app again, but Fi shook her head.

"Okay, just, don't interrupt me until I'm finished because I don't really know what I'm about to say," Fi blurted out.

Rowan bit her bottom lip but didn't say a word.

"I don't care about the camping trip." Fi saw Rowan's eyes get big, but she still kept silent. "I don't. I don't know why I cared so much about it in the first place, actually. I don't even *like* camping. I like soccer. And I like *Ducky McFowl*, even though I would rather die than tell my mom that. I like running to true crime podcasts even though that's totally creepy. I like my ridiculous siblings, even if they make me so, so angry. And . . ." Fi took a deep breath. "And I like *you*. You saved this con for Cat and Alex after I was, really, kind of a garbage older sister. And you saved the con for *me*. I was so set on hating everything here that I didn't even bother to see the good in it. And *you* showed that to me. You're not afraid to be exactly who you are, and neither is anyone else here. You taught me that this convention is *about* being exactly who you are, and about finding the people who love you for *you*. No matter what you love, someone else here loves it just as much. Probably more, actually. I've never been someplace where I can be sure that I'm not the weirdest person in the room. But also that all the other weirdos are probably kind of awesome. And . . ." Fi trailed off, suddenly embarrassed. "I don't know. That's it, I guess."

Rowan, who still had her phone out, lifted it a little bit higher. Fi heard the camera sound go off.

"What are you doing?" Fi asked, flustered.

"Item twenty-six," Rowan responded simply. She looked back down at her phone to submit it on the app.

Item twenty-six . . . Fi racked her brain. She'd looked at this like one zillion times today. What was item twenty-six?!

Rowan looked back up from her phone and smiled at Fi's unasked question. "'Submit a photo of the most beautiful thing at GeekiCon.'"

Before Fi even had a chance to register the blush that had surely spread from her hairline all the way down to her toenails, Rowan leaned in and kissed her on the cheek. Fi felt like the entire left side of her face was on fire. She was certain that Rowan could hear her heart pounding. Her hands were sweaty. Why did hands even get sweaty?!

Rowan pulled back and giggled—actually *giggled*—at the stunned look on Fi's face. "Yeah, even I have to admit that was pretty smooth."

That was enough to start Fi giggling, too. "It *really* was, what the heck!" Fi was laughing so hard now she was almost bent in two. Is this just what a day at GeekiCon did to you by the end of it?

Rowan was already back to business and had started talking about the Mystery Item again. Collecting herself, Fi finally put her hands on her knees and straightened herself up. People were still wandering around the *Lunar Soldier* sales section—no one had even noticed Fi and Rowan's little moment together. All the toys were so bright and colorful, and the posters—

The *posters*.

"Rowan," Fi said, interrupting her friend— *Friend? Girlfriend? Whatever, later*—but Rowan didn't seem to notice. "Rowan!" Fi repeated with more urgency. She tugged on the girl's sleeve and pointed upward. *"Look!"*

There, directly above the girls' heads, was a

giant *Lunar Soldier* poster hanging from the ceiling rafters and swaying in the breeze of the (very strong) convention air-conditioning. It showed five Planetary Soldiers all decked out in their finest, tiniest skirts, looking ready for battle or for a beauty tutorial, whichever came first.

And if you looked at the poster just right—from just the right angle, say directly below it—you would notice that one side of Lunar Soldier's crown was a little blurry.

And it looked *just* like the Mystery Item photo on the app.

"No way, dude," Rowan breathed.

"*Yes* way, dude!" Fi was jumping up and down now. "Get it! Get it!"

"Cat and Alex are *not* going to believe this." Rowan grinned as she snapped the photo.

"Oh." Fi grinned back. "You have *no idea*."

26. Submit a photo of the most beautiful thing at GeekiCon. (45 points)

25

Cat.

Could not.

Believe it.

First, she'd been like, *We're totally going to win.* And then she'd been like, *No, we're definitely going to lose.* But now, with Alex coming through like this at the last minute, she was like, *We might actually, totally, definitely, absolutely be able to win.*

Maybe.

Probably?

Seriously. And there was only one way to be sure.

Her hands shaking with nervous energy, Cat reached forward and pulled aside the black curtain separating their little hidden antechamber from what lay beyond.

Cat was hit with a wall of sound as her eyes adjusted to the darkness ahead of her. The echoey reverb of people talking on microphones in a massive room combined with the chatter of thousands of people enveloped her. Alex shoved her forward so they could drop the curtain back behind them, calling as little attention to their position as possible. Cat squinted as the crowd erupted into laughter, and the room finally came into clear focus.

Hall M. This was it. This was *it*. Cat had read about it for years online. This is where all the biggest announcements were made every single year at GeekiCon. It's where all the biggest stars from all the best geeky movies and TV shows came to chat with their fans. It's where any relative nobody could get up to the microphone and ask literal superheroes what they liked to eat for breakfast.

It was everything Cat had imagined. It was *more*.

The room itself was a "room" only in the sense that it had four walls and a ceiling. Really, it was more like a sports stadium. Over six thousand folding chairs covered the concrete floor in neat rows, separated by aisles for people to enter and exit as calmly as was possible in a place like this. It was as dark as a movie theater. At the front of the hall was a raised stage set with a loooong table. Movie stars sat along it, each with their own microphone, in front of GeekiCon's iconic backdrop. Usually, some awkward bro wearing a blazer over a T-shirt who wanted to look cool by association stood at a podium next to the table and asked the stars questions. For the six thousandth person in the back of the hall, gigantic screens on either side of the stage magnified the stars' faces. In the aisles, two microphones stood proudly on stands, guarded by lime-shirted volunteers. Excited fans lined up for hours—for days, even—for the chance to ask their faves a question.

"It's *Wormhole*," Cat breathed in disbelief. The cast of her *very favorite* Star *franchise were right up there onstage.* She couldn't believe her luck.

"C'mon," Alex hissed in Cat's ear, jarring her back to reality. "We should move!"

Cat shook her head. She had to remember why she was here. It *wasn't* to admire the cast of *Wormhole*, even though they were *right up there, holy Hannah*—it was to win the Quest.

Alex reached out his hand and Cat grabbed

it. Ducking to keep out of view, Cat sped as fast as she could toward the back of the hall. This far back, there were tons of empty seats—there might have been a huge line outside, but it was likely for the next panel or the one after that. *Wormhole* just didn't have the same audience it did while it was on the air.

Cat understood. It didn't bother her.

. . . Much.

Cat and Alex slid into two seats at the end of a row and put their heads together.

"I can't believe you got us in here," Cat whispered excitedly. She kept popping her head up to see Bradley Dan Anders up on the big screen. *BDA was really here!*

"Cat." Alex snapped his fingers in front of her face. Right. Quest. Right. Hall M.

"Right, sorry, yes." Cat pulled her phone out. "Okay, item eight: 'Cartwheel down the center aisle in Hall M.'"

"One hundred points," Alex finished for her.

"One. Hundred. Points," Cat confirmed. That was huge. Even if they weren't able to complete every item on the list—and it *was* getting late in the day—having a *one hundred point–item* in their pocket would go a long way toward launching them toward the top of the standings. So few people at GeekiCon actually got into Hall M to begin with—over 130,000 people came to the con, and the 6,500 who got into Hall M usually sat and refused to leave, which is like . . . math that Alex could probably do in his head. But the point was that not many people who go to GeekiCon got into this room, let alone people who were doing the Quest.

Or people who had the courage to do cartwheels down the center aisle.

"Can you cartwheel?" Alex asked, sounding suddenly panicked. "I can't believe I didn't ask that before. I didn't even think about it. What if neither of us can—?"

"Yes." Cat cut Alex off before he could start spiraling too hard. "It's okay. I can definitely, totally cartwheel. I've been practicing," she added proudly. It hadn't been going, like, *well*. But Alex didn't need to know that part. She was passable at the cartwheel game, and that's what mattered.

"Okay." Alex breathed out. "Okay. So I'll tape. And you cartwheel. Good."

"When should we do it?" Cat poked her head up again. The room was about half full. That was still many thousands of people. But it could have been worse.

"Between panels?" Alex suggested.

Cat shook her head. "The aisles will be full of people coming and going. You won't be able to get a clear shot. And I'll probably get trampled," she added as an afterthought.

"Okay, before that." Alex thought for a second, tapping his fingers on his jeans. "What about final question?"

"Yes!" Cat agreed, just a little too loudly. She clamped a hand over her mouth and reverted back to a whisper. "It's perfect. When the moderator says 'last question,' I'll get up. As soon as they're done answering and the cast starts leaving the stage, when everyone stars clapping, I'll do it. It'll be like my own standing ovation!"

"I like it, but . . ." Alex looked his sister straight in the eye. Cat swallowed. "Cat, just promise me you'll be careful—"

"Okay, we've got time for just one last question!" Cat's and Alex's heads snapped toward the screen on their side of the stage. The panel moderator's larger-than-life grin while stating something so obviously panic inducing made Cat dislike him more than she already did in principle.

"Get your camera out!" Cat gave Alex one last supportive thumbs-up before darting out into the aisle.

"Be careful!" she heard him whisper behind her—but Alex still followed her out into the aisle.

Cat stood at the back of the hall, opening and closing her fists at her side. As she danced from foot to foot, she noticed that her blisters weren't even hurting her anymore. She was officially too nervous to feel pain. Is this what it felt like to be Alex all the time?

Hall M stretched on and on in front of Cat, the aisle impossibly long and growing longer by the second. In front of the stage, the last fan asked their question at the microphone staffed by a volunteer. Cat's ears were roaring—she didn't hear the question, but the crowd and the panelists laughed. The moderator started wrapping up the panel. People were standing up and clapping as BDA and her beloved *Wormhole* cast got up to leave the stage.

This was it.

This was her moment.

The aisle was clear. It was now or never.

Cat threw her arms over her head and launched herself forward. The darkness of Hall M made the floor and ceiling almost indistinguishable from one another as Cat tumbled down the aisle, the room flying from upside down to right side up in seconds over and over and over again. Cat ignored the sounds of surprise from either side of the aisle. She just had to hope that Alex was catching her in all her glory. Seven cartwheels—now eight—now nine—how far was she from—?

"Cat!" She heard her brother's shouted warning but couldn't stop herself—her momentum was too strong. Cat's hands landed on the concrete in front of her, her legs swung over her head—and she crashed *right* into the microphone stand.

With the loudest amplified clatter ever heard in the history of humankind, Cat landed on her butt on the hard concrete floor, tangled in wire and mic stand. The lime-shirted volunteer stood next to her, and when Cat got her dizziness in check long enough to peer up, she saw that the volunteer looked horrified.

Cat grinned. "Sorry about that!"

The volunteer just stared.

Cat shrugged and stood up, rubbing her tailbone—*ouchhhhh*—but she was still caught in the mic wires. Cat hopped up and down on one foot while trying to unravel herself.

She heard Alex yell out for her again. "It's okay!" Cat called back, still distracted by the wire. "We did it! Upload the—"

"You won't be uploading *anything*."

Cat froze, still on one foot, her hands still tugging at the wire tangled around her midsection. She looked up slowly, catching herself just as she was about to tumble over.

James M. marched down the aisle, the back of Alex's shirt in one hand, her brother's phone in the other. Last time James M. had managed to capture Alex, her brother had looked distraught. Now, Alex just looked *furious*.

"Let him go," Cat said with as much menace as she could muster.

"You two," James M. spat out, reaching Cat while Alex still struggled to escape his grip, "are the *worst* part of GeekiCon."

"Did you mean you?" Alex shot back. James M. ignored him.

"You're both coming with me to the security office *right now*," James M. said, tucking Alex's phone into his back pocket. "And I am banning you from this convention. For *life*."

"Ah, that sounds great, really," Cat snarked, "but I'm a little tied up right now, so—"

"Enough!" James M. was turning bright red. He lurched forward and began yanking at the cords around Cat's shoulders, the mic itself swinging back and forth wildly across the floor. The commotion and the noise, projected over the hall's massive speaker system, was drawing a crowd. As Cat struggled to escape from both the mic and James M., people were gathering around them, standing between the seats on either side of the aisle.

"Get *off*—" Cat finally managed to spin herself free of the cord in James M.'s hand. Behind James M. and Alex, Cat saw a familiar figure burst from the ever-expanding crowd of gawkers. Late, as usual—the Gallo family way.

"Let him go!" Fi shouted, stopping in the aisle a few feet behind them. "Rowan, help—" Fi looked quickly from side to side. But she was alone. Her new friend was gone.

James M. twisted to look back at Fi. "How did you get in here?" he demanded, shocked.

Fi waved her badge in the air. "Amazing what having an important-looking badge and a smooth-talking friend can do for you."

James M.'s eyes narrowed. "You're *next*," he growled, before turning back and lunging for Cat's shirt. Cat danced back out of his reach. With a frustrated yell, James M. tugged on the cord one last time, the microphone sailing through the air and falling into his grip. Cat had never seen someone look so much like a supervillain in real life as this guy did right now. *Especially* since he still held on to the back of Alex's shirt with an iron grip.

"You listen to me, you little twerp," James M. hissed. He spoke quietly—the kind of angry quiet that was the most scary in parents and teachers alike. But it didn't matter; James M.'s voice came from all sides. The microphone in his hand made sure of that. Cat thought of the scene in the *Wormhole* finale when one of the angry gods came through the wormhole to destroy the Earth, voice booming. The Wormhole team had stood their ground then.

She would be just as brave now.

"You are the problem with this convention," James M.'s vitriol boomed, spit flying from the corners of his mouth. He kept stepping toward Cat, and she kept backing up.

"You don't understand what GeekiCon is *about*," James hissed. Cat was *very* aware that the stage was only a few more steps behind her—she was running out of places to run.

"You think it's about scavenger hunts and *shipping* and *politics*." He was getting closer.

"*Real fans* don't want that. This is *my* convention. *I'm* a *real fan*. And *real fans* don't like *forced diversity* and *cancerous feminism. Real* fans . . ." Cat's back hit the stage. This was it.

"*Real* fans like—"

"*Soccer.*" A voice even louder than James M.'s

took over the speaker system. "And I like *Ducky McFowl*, even though I would rather die than tell my mom that." Cat took her eyes off James M., just for a second. She *knew* that voice. "I like running to true crime podcasts even though that's totally creepy." Cat swung her head from side to side, searching for the source. "I like my ridiculous siblings, even if they make me so, so angry."

Fi. Of course that was Fi's voice. But Fi was right in front of Cat—staring up at the stage above Cat. How was this . . . ?

Taking a chance, Cat pushed her back off the stage wall and spun around. Sure enough, there was Fi *again*—her face magnified on either side of the stage to several hundred times its actual size. It was not her sister's best angle; it looked like someone had shot her from below with a shaky cell phone. But there was no doubt that the person on-screen was Fi.

"What is going *on*—?!" roared James M. But his microphone no longer worked, and his voice was drowned out by Fi's.

"I was so set on hating everything here that I didn't even bother to see the good in it," this giant version of her sister continued. The crowd was transfixed by it.

"Fi!" Cat yelled. "How are you doing this?"

"I'm not!" the real-life version of her sister shouted back over James M.'s head.

"This convention is *about* being exactly who you are, and about finding the people who love you for *you*," continued giant Fi. "No matter what you love, someone else here loves it just as much. Probably more, actually."

Cat caught Alex's eye in front of her. She winked at him. He winked back.

"I've never been someplace where I can be sure that I'm not the weirdest person in the room," giant Fi boomed. "But also that all the other weirdos are probably kind of awesome."

The video cut off.

The people in Hall M stared at the blank screens, stunned.

And then they erupted.

Every nerd in the room burst into cheers and applause. The crowd that had been gathering around James M. and the twins surged forward. Someone—Cat was *sure* it was the lime-shirted volunteer—ripped the microphone out of James M.'s hand. Someone else pushed between Alex and James M., severing their connection. In the massive, supportive crowd, Cat was able to become anonymous. The tidal wave of geeks swept James M. from the hall, shrieking. Cat raced through legs to grab her brother's hand—he didn't seem to mind, in this instance—and then Fi's. Together, the three of them ran for the curtained area to the right of the stage. In the crowd, no one noticed them slipping through.

"About time." There, behind the curtain, stood Rowan. Her face was lit by a multitude of glowing screens. Cat took in the scene around them—computers, audio boards, monitors—this must be the control center for the stage. Microphone volume, lighting controls, and . . .

"I know I shouldn't have taken video of you without asking," Rowan said apologetically, holding her phone up. "But I guess it came in handy."

Cat noticed Rowan's phone was attached to a cable that fed into one of the computers on the control panel. Rowan tapped her phone. Fi's face was suddenly back on every monitor.

Fi threw herself at Rowan and planted a kiss on the girl's cheek. *Ugh*, thought Cat. *Teenagers.*

Leaving them alone for a moment, Cat turned to her brother. "Are you okay?"

"I'm okay," Alex said with a small smile. "I can't believe he got me twice."

"I can't believe we got our Quest item!" Cat grinned—but the smile dropped off her face almost as soon as it appeared. "But—oh no. James M.—he had your phone! With the video!"

Alex pressed his lips together. He always did that when he had a secret.

"Spill it!" Cat urged.

"Okay, okay." Alex laughed. He pulled his phone from his pocket. "I grabbed it the second he put it in his pants pocket. I'm basically right at butt level. Gross, but in this case very helpful."

Cat burst out laughing. "Definitely, absolutely very helpful. Now, what are you waiting for?" She nudged her brother. "C'mon. It's time to upload."

8. Cartwheel down the center aisle in Hall M. (100 points)

26

"How do I look?" Alex asked his sister, nervously tugging on his bow tie. They were on their way to the Quest Masquerade, the big cosplay party where the winners of the Quest would be announced. Alex didn't really care that much about celebrities—besides Adrianna Tack and a few other comic-book artists—but even he had to admit that the idea of seeing Corwin Blake and all his *Paranormal* cast members in person was a *little* exciting.

He would never tell Cat as much. But yes. He was a little excited.

"You look great," Cat reassured him. She had changed out of her cape and into a party dress.

The fabric was printed with AC Comic strips from the '60s. Alex's bow tie was made out of the same material. They didn't feel like dressing up in full costumes after the day they'd had, so they decided to go geek stylish instead. But Alex wasn't used to wearing anything other than jeans and a T-shirt, so he still felt a little awkward.

"Is Mom already there?" Fi asked from behind them. She was walking beside Rowan and had finally ditched the coffee-stained blouse, donning a dress color coordinated to match Rowan's purple hair. They were holding hands.

Alex supposed that if he was going to have to put up with his sister dating someone, it might as well be someone as cool as Rowan.

"Yeah," Cat responded. They were walking down the streets of San Diego, the restaurants and shops all just as decked out in GeekiCon gear as they were. Alex saw Cat check her Google Maps and then her texts. Alex didn't need the map—he knew the restaurant right on the corner in front of them was the one they were aiming for. "Mom and Dad are—"

"*Sme tu!*" Alex's mom stood up from one of the tables outside the restaurant excitedly. Their dad stayed seated but looked just as happy to see them.

Alex watched as Cat launched herself into their mom's arms. While hugging, his mom waved over at him. Alex smiled and waved back. Moms always knew what to do.

"Mom, this is Rowan," Fi introduced, and Rowan and Alex's mom shook hands around Cat's head.

"Mrs. Gallo, I'm *such* a huge fan—"

"Thank you for taking care of my family today." Alex's mom laughed. "I hear you like *Ducky McFowl*?" They seemed to get along right away.

"Come on," their dad said, standing up. "Let's get inside. How did the Questing go?"

Cat started chattering away about their day while their mom spoke in rapid Slovak to Fi. She was getting dressed down but only a little. And Fi took it in stride. After all, she still had Rowan.

"You ready for this?" asked Rowan, as the six of them found a booth inside and sat down.

"I think so." Alex nodded. "We did our best today."

Rowan smiled. "You really did."

Alex looked around the restaurant and took in the full scope of the Masquerade. The costumes here were just as impressive as the ones he'd been seeing all day at GeekiCon, and everyone looked equally happy to be here. Old friends, new friends, internet friends, con friends—people ran excitedly over to one another to compliment their cosplays and Quest successes. Kids were taking tons of selfies, adults were gossiping, and the noise of the chatter in the place was almost as loud as the din in Hall M. Most of all, Alex just noticed the big smiles on the faces of every single person in the room. He wore one to match, without even thinking about it.

"Are you Team DoubleTrouble?" A girl had rushed over to their table dressed like a companion from *Whom, M.D.*

"Yes—I love your costume!" Alex responded.

"Thanks, I love Delaney sooo much!"

"She's my favorite companion!" Alex said excitedly.

"Me, too!" The girl did a twirl, her skirt floating up. "I just wanted to say I saw your item twenty-five on the Quest app. So sweet!"

Alex frowned. "We didn't get to item twenty-five."

"But *we* did." Alex's mom leaned over in the booth to join in the conversation. "'Pass a hat around a crowded panel and collect donations for charity. The panelists must sing until the hat has reached every person in the room.' We did it in the *Ducky McFowl* panel. But by then, you and your sister had already . . . absconded."

Alex blushed. He would have to look that word up later. "Thank you," he said to his mom. He turned back to the Delaney cosplayer. They exchanged social media handles and vowed to get in touch later.

So maybe the crowds at GeekiCon weren't *all* bad. At least, not the people *in* them.

25. Pass a hat around a crowded panel and collect donations for charity. The panelists must sing until the hat has reached every person in the room. (83 points)

27

Fi squeezed Rowan's hand under the booth. Yeah, she'd gotten chewed out by her mom, as anticipated—but really, it wasn't so bad. And her mom *had* been stoked to find out that Fi was finally gaining an appreciation for the nerdier things in life, also as anticipated. Plus, Rowan had babbled so many compliments about *Ducky McFowl* within, like, the first thirty seconds of meeting her mom that there was no *way* she had been able to stay angry. It was perfect.

Not caring about the camping trip anymore also meant Fi didn't have to worry about having lost the twins for several hours today. It was totally fine. And she had someone to sit with at lunch now, regardless.

Rowan felt the hand squeeze. She looked over at Fi and gave her a secret smile. Fi felt herself go red all over again.

"Wait," Cat said suddenly, and everyone in their booth turned to look at her. "We can have four Quest team members. If Alex and I were doing it . . . and Mom . . . and Fi and Rowan . . ." Alex watched Cat count them all off on her fingers. "That's one too many! We'll be disqualified!"

"Oh, don't worry," Rowan piped up from next to Fi. "Only Fi registered on the app. I was just her cheerleader. She found all the items."

Fi thought back on it and realized Rowan was right. "Guess I didn't need your help after all!"

The table's laughter was cut short by the restaurant's lights dimming. A spotlight came up on a makeshift stage in the back of the venue. The whole room exploded into shrieks as *Paranormal* star Corwin Blake stepped out onto the platform, waving at the crowd. He was just as handsome and roguish in real life as he was on the show, his hair just as artfully messy, his eyes just as deep.

Not that Fi would know anything about the

show. She'd just . . . seen it on her sister's laptop a couple of times. That was all.

Really!

Fi leaned over to shout in Rowan's ear over the noise of Corwin and the crowd. "Thank you for today!"

Rowan shook her head. "For what?"

"For everything!" Fi yelled back. "For showing me there's nothing wrong with being a weirdo—as long as you're a happy weirdo!"

Rowan burst out laughing. "For that, you're so, so welcome." Rowan squeezed Fi's hand in return. "I'll be right back!"

Fi nodded and watched as Rowan slid out of the booth, her purple hair disappearing around a corner. Fi still had a smile on her face. Happy weirdos might just, in fact, rule.

28

"That's Corwin Blake!" Cat squealed with excitement.

"I know!" Alex yelled back.

"He's so cute!"

"Gross!" Alex shook his head. Cat just laughed. Her favorite *Paranormal* star was right up there . . . Things were good with Alex . . . Everything was as it should be.

"And now," Corwin drawled from the stage. People of every gender in the crowd hung off his every word. He absolutely, positively *was* that cute. "The announcement you've all been waiting for."

Cat's breath caught in her throat. She felt her

foot start bouncing up and down against the booth. This was it. *This* was the moment! Alex reached out and grabbed Cat's hand. They were in this together.

"The winners," Corwin said, drawing it out, "of Quest Year Five . . . *are* . . ."

Cat froze. Could it be . . . ?

"Team Dangermaker!"

The crowd applauded. The blood rushed back into Cat's head.

They'd lost.

Team Dangermaker had won.

Again.

Cat felt a hand squeeze her thigh and looked over into her mom's smiling face. "You did so good," her mom reassured her. "You should be proud of yourself!"

Cat clapped a few times, halfheartedly. She *was* happy for Team Dangermaker . . . she just *really* thought they'd had it this time. She watched as the four members of Team Dangermaker bounded up to the stage to claim their trophy from Corwin; there went Dahlia and Malik. The white teenager who followed them must have been Fox. And then Rey—

"Holy sh—"

"Fi!" her mother scolded. "Language!"

"No," Cat interjected, standing up in her seat. "She's right—look!"

Clambering up onto the stage was the fourth member of Team Dangermaker.

Rowan.

Cat kept looking back and forth between Fi and the stage, her head whipping back and forth so fast she got dizzy and had to sit down again. Fi was just staring straight ahead.

"But she never said anything . . ."

"But her name is Rowan." Cat slammed her hands on the table. "Not Rey."

Fi dropped her head down to the table in front of her and mumbled something. Cat picked Fi up by the scruff of her dress.

"Again," Cat urged.

"Rowan," Fi repeated, understandable this time. "Rowan *Reyes*."

Cat dropped the back of Fi's dress and stared at the stage, wide-eyed. "So *that's* why she never technically helped us."

"And why she knew so much about the Quest," Fi agreed.

"You're dating someone *famous*," Alex chimed in. Fi just blinked.

"*Nerd* famous," Cat agreed. "You're basically nerd royalty now. Congratulations, Queen of the Nerds."

"*Bože môj.*" Their mom shook her head, still clapping for the winning team.

"But wait," Corwin said into the mic, bringing the room back down to a hush. "There's more!"

Cat sat back up in her seat. More?

"Some of you may have noticed a Mystery Item was added to the Quest list today." Cat slumped back down. She and Alex hadn't found it. And if Fi and Rowan had found it, Rowan obviously would have uploaded it on behalf of Team Dangermaker. Cat examined her nails to distract herself from her sinking feeling of disappointment.

"We are thrilled to announce that one team—*just one*—managed to find the secret item." *Whatever.* "Come get your prize—" *Whatever.* ". . . Team DoubleTrouble!"

Whatever.

Wait.

What?

Fi was shaking Cat's shoulder. "That's us! Go! Go!"

Cat stumbled out of the booth with Alex beside her. "What happened?"

"We found it!" Fi laughed. "I found it! We won!"

Cat couldn't believe what she was hearing. She couldn't believe this was happening. She walked forward, half in a dream, to the stage, where someone reached down a hand to help her off the ground.

Cat looked up. The hand was attached to Corwin Blake.

She put her hand in his. It was the best-looking hand she'd ever touched. She would never wash it again in her entire life. Did you even know they made eyes that *dark*?!

"Congratulations, Team DoubleTrouble." Corwin pumped his fist in the air and the crowd cheered. Cat turned and stared out into the restaurant in shock. This was real. This was really happening!

"As a reward for your excellent detective skills and your otherwise impressive Quest score," Corwin said as Cat stared up at him in awe, "you'll be having dinner with the *Paranormal* cast and crew tomorrow. We've brought out all the stars, our directors, writers, and even our art director! Congratulations, Team DoubleTrouble!"

Cat looked over at her brother in shock as the room exploded into applause yet again. She knew that the expression on his face must have matched the one on hers. Dinner?! With Corwin Blake?! A chance for Alex to talk to their art director?! This was more than Cat ever could have imagined.

Alex flung out his arms and Cat threw herself into them. Together, they jumped in a circle around the stage, Corwin Blake laughing behind them. Out of the corner of her eye, Cat saw Fi run over to Team Dangermaker to sweep Rowan up in a huge hug, too.

They did it. They *did it*. Cat didn't want to jinx herself, but . . .

"Best. Con. *Ever*," she yelled in Alex's ear.

"Best. Con. *Ever!*" he yelled right back.

Well. Not *quite*. Cat looked over one more time at Fi and Rowan with a renewed sense of determination.

Yep. It was time to start planning for next year!

Tips for Having An I-CON-ic Con Experience!

Do you want to hit up a comic convention of your very own, just like Cat and Alex? You should—they're amazing! Here are some fun tips for getting your con on:

- Ask your adults to help you find a con in your area. There are so many comic conventions out there now, so chances are great that there's a con within a couple hours' drive of your house! (P.S. Sometimes you get in for free if you're under twelve. Aww yiss.)
- Check out the convention's website ahead of time to scope out who's going to be there, what you want to do, and who you want to see. Con guests can range from the legit famous (like TV and movie actors) to the lesser known (but no less cool) nerd variety (like comic book writers and artists).
- You can meet guests at autograph and photo sessions, or you can see them speak on panels. If you go for an autograph or photograph, prepare something you want to say in advance, just in case you get nervous in the moment. You'll be ready!
- Dress up! If you want to go full cosplay (dressing up in costume), that's *awesome*. If not, wear your favorite

geeky T-shirt to let everyone know which fandom is your number one. Still awesome!

- Pack a backpack with your essentials for the day, and don't forget to include a book or a portable console. Sometimes, lines for panels or autographs can be really long, and you don't want to get bored. Make sure you leave space for anything you might buy, or bring a folded-up cloth bag for any bigger purchases!

- Wear comfy shoes—you're going to be walking on concrete floors all day, so a good sneaker is a must. And pack a healthy lunch and snacks—apples and a refillable bottle of water are always good bets!

- Bring a camera, or stick close to someone with a camera! There are endless opportunities for fun photo ops, from LEGO statues to mega lines. If you see someone in a cool costume and you want a photo with them, just remember to ask politely first!

- Go see a panel you know nothing about! You might learn something cool and leave as a fan of someone new.

- Visit Artist Alley and come home with a small souvenir from a local artist! You'll be supporting someone's comics career, and you'll never forget your first con.

- Many cons have a Kids' Day! There are tons of fun activities—I've seen everything from wand dueling to comic creating. Kids' Days tend to be on Sunday, the final day of most cons, which is also a less busy day on the floor—and when lots of booths are trying to get rid of the rest of their goodies. You might even get something cool for free!

Acknowledgments

Here we are, at a place I never in a million years imagined I would be: the acknowledgments page for my first *novel*. I've been fortunate enough to have written some pretty neat stuff in my career, from comics to nonfiction books to video games; but there's something about writing a *novel* that's always felt like an impossibility to me. Writing novels is something *other* people did, people smarter and more gifted and in tune with *the muse* than I.

And yet, here we are. As it turns out, I *could* do it. And if *I* could do it, that means *you*, reader (yes, you!), absolutely could, too. And I hope you do! No one else can tell your story—and I want to read it.

But I didn't write this novel alone! As always, I would be nowhere without my incredible agent, Maria Vicente, who had faith in my writing long before I did. It's been wonderful to watch her career blossom, and I'm so grateful to have her as my partner on this weird and wild writing journey.

Con Quest! itself was brought to life with the advice and assistance of my brilliant editor Weslie Turner. Her enthusiasm for this project (and her deep love for Gen Con!) helped steer this book in the best possible direction. I'm so grateful for the patience, kindness, and guidance she showed me as a first-time novelist. I also owe a huge debt of gratitude to my original editor, Rhoda Belleza, who dreamed up *Con Quest!* and who took a chance on me as its writer. Go read her *Empress of a Thousand Skies*, because it rules!

Truly, the entire team at Imprint has been a dream to work with. Erin Stein and John Morgan, it's been great to meet you . . . at cons. Ha! To them, and to managing editors Dawn Ryan and Hayley Jozwiak, production managers Raymond Ernesto Colón and Jie Yang, copy editor Kathleen Scheiner, and the rest of the Imprint team, thank you for all of your hard work and support over the last two and a half years. Thank you also to our ASD sensitivity reader, Lyn Miller-Lachmann, for your wonderful advice on bringing Alex to life (and your great LEGO knowledge!). And have you seen how cool this book looks?! Chris Danger and Natalie Sousa, you crushed it. Thank you for your time and your talent.

Con Quest! is based largely on my own experience competing in a massive, nerdy, world-wide scavenger hunt, so I must thank my ridiculous and amazing GISH team, the Trash Pandas: Andrea D., Emma L., Esti P., Kimberley B., Kristin L., Meg S., Rachel W., Sarah, Scott W., Stacey D., Mia S., Angela V., Erick B., Lisa J., and all of Stacey's tarantulas. I still can't believe Meg wore an all-vegetable cheerleader outfit in public. #blessed

There would be no book at all without the love and support of my best friends: my family (*awwwwwwww, barf!!*). My mom was my very first convention buddy, and our biannual trips to Gatecon are still my favorite trips in the world. I would (and do) fly across the world for her Slovak cabbage noodles. My dad made me a nerd to begin with, and I wouldn't have this career had he not been willing to pull me out of school in the sixth grade to go see *The Phantom Menace*. (We'll get you to San Diego, Dad . . . one day!). And my amazing, supportive, kind, nerdy husband(!): Blair made sure I ate and slept and generally survived the writing of this book and never once complained about my absurd work schedule. I love you all so much. The best geeks a gal could possibly ask for.

And to you, my reader! Embrace your wacky, your weird, your wonderful. I hope to see you at a con sometime soon!

About the Author

Sam Maggs is a bestselling writer of books, comics, and video games including *Marvel Action: Captain Marvel, The Unstoppable Wasp: Built on Hope, Tell No Tales*, and *Marvel's Spider-Man* for the Playstation 4. Her work has taken her to comic book conventions all over the world. A Canadian in Los Angeles, she misses Coffee Crisp and bagged milk. *Con Quest!* is her debut middle-grade novel. Visit her online at sammaggs.com or @SamMaggs.